THIS IS N

With Love,
Savi

THIS IS NOT YOUR STORY

SAVI SHARMA

westland publications ltd

61, II Floor, Silverline Building, Alapakkam Main Road, Maduravoyal, Chennai 600095

93, I Floor, Sham Lal Road, Daryaganj, New Delhi 110002

First published by westland ltd 2017

10 9 8 7 6 5 4 3 2

ISBN: 978-93-86224-39-2

Designed by SÜRYA, New Delhi

Printed at Thomson Press (India) Ltd

Savi Sharma asserts the moral right to be identified as the author of this work.

This novel is entirely a work of fiction. The names, characters and incidents portrayed in it are the product of the author's imagination. Any resemblance to actual persons, living or dead, or events or localities is entirely coincidental.

Dedicated to

YOU, AGAIN

'Remember, there is a cost for every story in your life.
A cost for making your story better,
A cost for not making your story better.
And it's you who will have to pay for it.
So decide carefully, what you want.
Which story you want to tell.'

Prologue

For a moment, forget who you are. More importantly, leave behind who we are and empty out everything. Instead, just be me.

'I never wanted anything from life.'

If I say those words, I would be lying. In fact, that would be the biggest lie of my life. I wanted, I have always wanted. I just never could bring the words out. My voice failing, my heart breaking, my soul shattering.

But, what do I really want in life?

I don't know yet. So, I will tell you everything I wanted and still want. Today, I will be true; true to you, and most importantly, true to myself.

I … I … I want to live.

Yes. Not one but many lives in one lifetime. I want to write about myself and everyone I ever met, capture the essence of what it's like to live. To be able to read everything beautiful and painful ever written and appreciate the experiences captured. All of this hoping to inspire and be inspired.

I want to learn and to teach. Yes, both, because I have had life-defining encounters that need to be shared and understood. Even so, I still have life-changing experiences, lessons to learn.

I want to give away everything I have. Yes, I want that and I want to begin again. To remind myself what it means to start over, to be back at the beginning of one's life.

I want to eat and dress well, have a nice car and a nicer home. To be rich, famous and appreciated. The little things and the bigger things, I want all of them.

I want to be single and yet attached. Alone yet accompanied. I want to be everything and nothing, all at once!

I want Death to want me. He cannot take me, I want him to come when I have exhausted these lives I want to live and become! I want him to desire the enriched soul I will be!

I want it all; slowly, gradually, definitely. But is this all possible? Can one person be all these things in one lifetime?

I don't know, but I certainly want to know.

FOUR YEARS AGO

1

SHAURYA

Jaipur

I was excited at the thought of sharing my dreams with
my parents. My mom has always been a loving and gentle
woman. A petite woman — far shorter than my dad and
I — she was encouraging of what I did for the most part,
and put my own wellbeing far above her own many times.
Housework, cooking, and attending to me made her
content. Her smile never failed to cheer me up, and the
contrast she held to her husband, my dad, was like a light
at the end of a long, dark tunnel. She created warmth, and
with a kiss she could cure a child's injury without ever
expecting a thank you for the miracles of motherhood that
she performed.

As for my dad, he was an orthodox man in both
appearance and action. He was a firm believer in letting

things off your chest, but he was infamous for asking questions that made you second-guess your decisions. I would cringe at the thought of not meeting his approval in my choices and actions. The intense stare from those brown eyes would hit me, making me feel as if my belly was flopping down onto the cold, marble floor. His mouth would move with precision to slam me with questions to encourage me to think things through. I knew that this was his way of showing me he cared about my future, but his questions stripped me of creativity, imagination, and, more times than I could count, my dreams as a child and adult. His words fell from his lips in two manners: an elected official, or a priest.

Sitting across the table from him added to the anxiety wrapping itself around the joints of my knees and elbows. My mom's spoon clacked against the pot with each scoop she served on the plates before us. She settled in her seat, and I remembered to breathe for a second. In my head I was trying to figure out how to start. Do I ask for their attention first? Or should I just blurt out my dream? No, maybe I should at least announce where I plan to go. My decision does require that I leave Jaipur, leave them far behind. The thudding of my heart made my chest ache; my palms were cold with sweat, and again I had to remind myself to breathe. Had I only taken two breaths since I'd sat at the dinner table under my dad's watchful eye?

'Mom, Dad.' It had taken me weeks to build up the courage to make the announcement. 'I want to go to Mumbai.'

The clanking of my dad's silverware against his plate made me flinch. 'Why on earth would you need to go to Mumbai?'

It was more abrasive of a reaction than I was prepared to face. The way his face reddened, the vein pulsing on his forehead and the sharpness of his stare cut me down with precision. He made it clear with his reaction that there was no reason for me to even think of Mumbai as a place I could go. Worse, clenching my fists under the table, I knew deep down the reaction wouldn't improve when I stated why I wanted to go there. I managed somehow to cling on to my courage to survive that moment and carry on.

'I ...' Swallowing, I pulled my courage back beside me before it could flee. 'I want to go there and take a filmmaking course, become a film director.'

'That's no path for people like us,' he grunted, and returned to the aggressive cutting of his food. 'A career like that is all about luck. It's a fool's dream.'

'And why do you need to go to Mumbai for that?' My mom had paused in her own eating. 'Can't you take classes here in Jaipur? On the side?'

'Mumbai has the best classes.' I had locked eyes with my dad, sweat trickled down the side of my neck. 'There are more opportunities to land a job afterwards in Mumbai as well.'

'I see.' My dad took a bite and chewed on it before continuing his interrogation. 'Shaurya, have you considered the cost of living in Mumbai?'

It was one of the practical questions I had prepared myself for. 'I am aware of that, Dad. In fact, I have been saving up for some time. My plan is to take the train to Mumbai. I have an idea of a few places within walking distance of the college I wish to attend, and —'

'And how do you know this college will accept you?' He lifted an eyebrow at me, another bite of food sliding into his mouth.

'I have been building up a portfolio …' I was losing my stand in the conversation. 'The photos I have been taking, those have been for me to prove my artistic eye.'

'With that old camera?' snorted my mom. 'But why on earth would a film college be interested in photos?'

I sighed, feeling like they were working together to spin me in circles. 'It's more than just filming something. You have to be able to tell a story, capture emotion, even in a single frame.'

'And how many are you competing against for jobs?' my dad took the reins again, laying his spoon down. 'How many jobs are there? Are you sure you'll be able to find one?'

'There are not as many as ...' I stopped myself, rephrasing my words. 'There are more jobs in Mumbai for filmmakers than anywhere else in India.'

'You seem unsure about this.' He went back to eating, as if confident he had redirected me on the matter. 'You should start preparing for your Chartered Accountancy entrance, Shaurya.'

My chest tightened. 'But, it's not what I want to do. My dream is to be a filmmaker.'

'I understand.' A swallow from his glass, and then he cleared his throat. 'Why mess with success? Why take a chance of failing?'

'I ...' My words failed me and I found myself out of answers.

My soul was ripped away from me, and with it my courage. I stared down at my plate; my appetite had gone and the taste in my mouth was sour with the words '*people like us*'. I didn't want to be a *person like this*. I wanted to chase after something that made me happy to wake up every morning. Was it so wrong to want to be something more?

Frustrated, I excused myself from the table. In the darkness of my bedroom I let the anger swirl in my mind. My dad had no idea what skill and talent was needed to become a film director. *A fool's dream?* Wasn't it foolish to be satisfied with a life that would not prosper beyond where it sits? To remain unhappy and miserable to the end of your days? My stomach twisted yet again, the idea of it all too nauseating to fathom. Becoming a filmmaker was no different from putting in the hard work and skills needed to become a CA. Being a CA — that was my dad's dream for me. Not mine.

My door cracked open. It was my mom.

'Shaurya, are you all right?' she smiled, inviting herself into the room. 'You barely ate.'

'I lost my appetite after Dad trampled on my dreams,' I said, glaring at her. 'What were your thoughts on the matter?'

'I have to admit, it's a silly idea.' She had the nerve to giggle at me. 'You should listen to your dad. He's a wise man, after all.'

Sitting up, my eyes ending the laughter, I warned, 'One day, I will be gone. I will hop onto a train to Mumbai and chase my dreams.'

I meant every word. As many times as I'd gone to the railway station, I could have been gone from here. I lifted the black photo frame from the wall, removed the photo in it, and replaced the empty frame. My mom made a face, lifting an eyebrow at the awkward moment.

Laying back down, I hissed, 'That will be my reminder that my destiny is an empty one. That my dreams mean nothing ...'

She sighed and turned on her heel to leave as she waved a hand in rebuttal. 'Stop being so dramatic, Shaurya. None of us ever gets to see our dreams …'

2

ANUBHAV

Jaipur

Growing up in Jaipur was something precious to me. Jaipur is a wonderful place to start one's life, amidst beautiful relics in the form of palaces, forts and even temples. Before our time, this was a place full of dreams coming true, and as a child, I wanted a piece of that.

My mom once asked me, 'What do you want to be when you grow up, Anubhav?'

I replied, 'A king of my own making.'

When I thought about it much later, it made me laugh to think of my tiny voice saying those big words; I didn't even know exactly what they meant. I do remember that my dad got a good laugh out of it. But never did my parents say no or correct the thought. After all, I was only a child at the time.

Dreams of being in my own tower of power built from something I had worked hard at, I suppose, was a worthy goal in life.

'Why Bangalore?' When I told my mom I wanted to move for my studies, her face was showing her age by that point. I looked at her eyes, suddenly sad at the thought of my leaving.

'Because one of the best colleges for pursuing MBA is there,' I smiled, reassuring her that this was indeed something I wanted to do, where I wanted to go. 'If I am going to build a successful business, then I should learn what I can from the very best, right?'

'He has a point.' My dad's eyes squinted as his grin grew wider, pushing his wrinkled cheeks high. 'We want the best for you as well, Anubhav.'

'I …' Tears danced in her eyes; she sniffled, gathering her words again. 'I will miss you terribly, Anubhav.'

Taking my mom into my arms, I was thankful they wouldn't keep me from going. 'I plan to get my MBA and launch a startup company while I am there. Please say you'll visit me in Bangalore.'

'Of course!' She pulled away, wiping the tears from her cheeks. 'Know that you are always welcome to come home if things don't work out.'

'I hope you find everything you are looking for,' my dad grunted, fighting back his own emotions. 'Make me proud, son.'

'I will. I know I will,' I nodded.

A few weeks later, I caught the train to Bangalore and — without a second thought — left Jaipur behind to pursue a Master's in Business and launch my startup venture.

~

Bangalore

Bangalore was an interesting place, not like Jaipur, yet reminiscent of Jaipur with large, towering skyscrapers leaving a sensation of modern palaces and temples. It seemed like the streets were crowded day and night. So much so, you wondered if the people there ever slept. They had their fair share of temples and relics, but they felt like weeds growing between the cracks of a brick road. Take a wrong turn, and you would find yourself in slums. The modern architecture there was amazing. You could find yourself standing in the streets, looking up in awe at the engineering needed to create a work of art people were able to live in, work in.

'You again?' The man blinked at me and came to stand by me, looking in the same direction I was, curious. 'I see you out here all the time, just staring up.'

'Does it not inspire you to see what someone designed, created from their imagination?' I eyed the man; he worked in the building I was gazing at, though I had never looked any deeper than that. 'And for you to work inside a work of art must be amazing.'

He chuckled. 'I've never thought of it that way. It was always *where I worked*. I suppose there *is* a great pride to it, to be in this extraordinary building.'

A smile crept across my face and with great confidence I claimed, 'One day I'll have my own business and join you in there.'

He folded his arms and grinned. 'Tell me about what you do,' he invited. 'I have a couple of minutes. I'd love to hear your story.'

My smile was bright as I took in his words. 'I like that. My story.'

I gestured to a low stone wall a few steps away and we sat down together. 'I have always wanted to be a successful entrepreneur. Although I am from Jaipur, my parents encouraged me to come to Bangalore to go to college and start my own venture.'

He nodded. 'You are lucky to have such supportive parents.'

'Yes, I am,' I mused. 'They gave me the courage to follow my dreams. I can barely wait to finish my degree — I have so many great ideas to bring to the world!'

'You are a fortunate young man,' he commented. 'You have both courage and support. That is a powerful combination, because both feed off each other. As long as you have both those things, I know your path will lead you to success.'

His words were as powerful as a bolt of lightning. 'Thank you,' I said. 'I look forward to the day you and I can have lunch together in this building.'

'For your sake, I hope your wish comes true.' He glanced at his wristwatch then and said, 'So sorry, I'll be late if I dream beside you any longer!'

Personally, I liked the buildings in India's Silicon Valley. Looking back later, maybe it was also the innovation of the businesses there that added to the curves and angles of the buildings. The outer shells of successful ideas decorated to match the greatness of the men and women achievers within those glass and concrete walls.

In this place, my creativity and determination were fuelled beyond what I could have hoped. The Amer Fort, where my parents often took me when I was kid, was far away, but in front of me were the palaces of modern man, ready for me to stake my own claim in them.

My dream was to be a successful entrepreneur, to become someone who could come out of my ordinary existence to bloom into something far greater.

PRESENT DAY

3

SHAURYA

Jaipur

The voices of travellers in the railway station washed over the platform like the murmuring of a river. To me, it was a numbing tone, much like silence. The red and yellow numbers flashing over the platform could not break me from the weight of my thoughts. They were nothing more than the pulsing beacons of the emotions wrestling with one another at the centre of my soul. Winter was ending, but it brought no cool breeze to make the long waits less agonizing as trains unloaded and loaded in screeching waves. February was being shy, keeping the last gentle cold fronts hidden and denying me the chill I should have been feeling at this moment. I weaved my way around the pillars and the occasional vendor, following the steps I had taken so often. There, as always on Platform No. 2, was an empty bench waiting, ever faithful, for me.

Sitting there alone, I was terrified and excited. The empty track before me would soon be filled with the metallic caterpillar promising to take me to a place where my dreams and ambitions could become reality. Stepping on board the train, I would be joining it on its journey, ready for the metamorphosis it had offered to so many before me. But my indecisiveness lay bitter in my mouth: was I willing to leave behind my parents — especially my mom, whom I adored so much — without regret?

All I wanted was the encouragement from them for me to reach for my dreams. Their responses, always in the back of my mind, brought on a drowning sensation now, and filled me with terror. Could I really leave everything behind? Would my life be happy without them there to share it all with? To bring a sense of pride to my parents and family would fill me with joy, wouldn't it? It should, but the idea of it all felt so lonesome and cold. Perhaps, today, I might finally be able to move from this bench and into the next chapter of my own story.

'May I sit here?' A middle-aged man cut through my thoughts, making me flinch.

'Y-yes.' The loneliness of my situation was still biting at my mind, and I saw no harm in allowing him to join me in this isolated nook.

The man eyed me for a moment before he spoke. 'This is my first time riding a train to Mumbai. How much longer will the train be?'

'Twenty minutes.' I didn't need to look at a clock; this was not my first time at the Mumbai platform.

'So, this is the Mumbai Platform No. 2?' He looked around, seeming lost, staring at the yellow flashing signs.

'Yes, you are on the right platform.' Straightening myself, I pointed across the way. 'That is Platform No. 3, where a train from Mumbai will arrive to unload. Here on Platform No. 2, the train going to Mumbai will arrive. If you intend to go to Mumbai, you are sitting in the right spot, sir.'

'Ah.' He nodded to himself, looking over the railway station in its entirety. 'So, are you going to Mumbai as well, my friend?'

I opened my mouth to answer, but hesitated. Part of me was screaming yes, while the other half was shouting no. This bench was still holding me down with the chains of my frustrations.

Swallowing back my thoughts, I mumbled my answer. 'Maybe ...'

The man's silence stung. Could he hear my thoughts? Could he feel my struggle between my life now and the life of my dreams?

'Maybe?' he repeated, a sense of surprise in his voice, but I said nothing. 'What do you do?'

'I am doing my CA, final year.' My reply felt dry, but I was happy to change topics.

'It's a good profession.' He was trying his best to change the mood between us, though I was not interested in brightening it myself. 'Your life will be set once you clear it. When are your final exams?'

Sighing, I replied, 'In three months.'

'Oh! How many attempts did it take you to reach the finals?' he asked, perking up, intrigued to know more.

'Cleared the entrance and IPCC, everything on first attempt.' I glanced at the man from the corner of my eyes, taking in his crow's feet. 'Now I just need to sit for my first attempt at the finals.'

'That's great!' he smiled at me, the creases on his face growing deeper in his joy on hearing my achievements. 'You will surely clear the finals! Live a great life!'

My gaze fell to the ground with a mix of emotions. 'We'll see ...'

'Why do you say that?' he asked gently.

'My parents ... this is the path they want me on,' I admitted.

'But it is not the one you would choose?'

'No.'

He sighed, leaned back and threaded his fingers behind his head, thinking carefully. Finally, he spoke again. 'I can tell you, others have tried to push me in other directions; paths of their choosing, not mine. I am a pig-headed man, I admit, and when this happened, their attempts to influence me only made me want even more to go in the opposite direction.'

'Truly?' I grinned, picturing my companion digging his heels into the ground like a stubborn mule.

'Yes,' he smiled. 'You have to tell yourself that the misery you fear your parents may inflict if you cross them will never be as bad as the misery that you are in by not standing up for your dreams. If you follow the path you wish, if you chase down those dreams, you will truly not suffer. It is what the universe genuinely wants you to do. Embrace this second chance and take back your dreams.'

Thoughts were creeping back into place, my heart aching. I was torn between love and duty. Was it always this difficult to follow both in one's life? The man was still trying to pry a conversation from me, but I was more alone than ever. His words drifted through my ears, in and out again like loose stitches on a hemline. On occasion, I muttered a monotonous answer to the endless queries he pitched at me. Here I was again, sitting on this bench, trying to decipher what I should do with my life. What did I want to do, what was it I needed to be? Who could I not leave behind in Jaipur?

'Life's a funny thing, you know?' The man leaned back on the bench, his eyes looking off to some invisible distance. 'If you don't give all of yourself to the life you want, heart, soul and mind, you won't go anywhere at all. Many times

I've found myself stuck, a lot like you are here, on this bench, unable to move no matter how much I yearned to go to that next chapter in my life.'

He had caught my attention. 'So what do you do when you get stuck?'

He chuckled, pleased to have me back in the conversation. 'I give it what it asks of me. I take risks, especially if the worst that can happen changes nothing from where I was sitting.'

'You seem so confident,' I said, my eyebrows raised high, feeling sceptical at his words. 'Risks can often land you in a far worse situation.'

'True,' he nodded, his grin widening. 'But then again, the weight of regret and asking yourself *what if,* down the road, is far more haunting to one's soul. What if I took that chance? Well, if the worst that happens is that you have to come back home and pick up where you left off, at least you can stop wasting time on dreaming and wondering if it's still a possibility.'

I took in his advice, mulling it over in my head. 'Still, isn't all that terrifying? What would your family think? Coming home to a family disappointed in you ...'

'Ah, but that's part of taking that leap of faith.' He leaned forward again. 'Remember, there is a cost for everything you want in life. A cost for making your life better, a cost for not making your life better. And it's you who will have to pay for it. So, decide carefully what you want.'

The screeching of a train on the tracks halted the man's words. My eyes shot up, taking in the doors of the train to Mumbai.

The man stood and took a step. Then he stopped and turned. 'Are you coming?'

Eyes locked on those doors, I was too afraid to say an answer aloud in the fear that it would make my decision final.

A horn blared, sounding the warning that the train would pull away soon. 'Young man, are you coming?'

I held my breath, a cold sweat coming over me.

'What are you thinking?' the man whispered, or perhaps my ears and mind were too far away to hear him now. 'The train is leaving, come …'

It was enough to prompt me to stand, my heart thumping in my ears. Still, my legs wouldn't move. Another long, hard whistle, the rumbling of the engine rising, and then the railway coaches were rocking into motion; the train was leaving. The man huffed at me, his lips folded in a scowl. His happy demeanour lost as my body, mind and soul wrestled with one another. A hissing sound hit my ears, making the train take on a monstrous tone. My throat tightened and I gave the man a look of helplessness. Why was it so hard to take even one step towards my dreams?

He had spoken to me of risks and leaps of faith, but I was still afraid to even take the smallest of steps. To come to the edge of this moment in my life had taken courage, and I still didn't know where it came from. But if I could truly be brave, like this man, perhaps I could be the one sitting and smiling at the bench. No, I lacked the ability to take blind leaps. Oh, how I knew the weight of regrets he'd spoken about, and the nightmare of playing the screaming chant of *What If.* Could today be the day I took a step towards my ambitions?

Sorrow swelled inside me as the man turned on his heel. He took off, sprinting in a frantic manner, and his shoulder slammed into a young woman. I opened my mouth to shout after him, but fear silenced what would have come out. He gave me a last pitiful look over his shoulder, and then hopped onto the metal beast. Motionless, I watched the train to Mumbai screech and snort further away.

Papers that the girl had been holding fell all around me, like a cold winter's snow. Goosebumps rippled across my skin. The sounds of the train, the girl's complaints, and even my thoughts fell silent. I was alone, swallowed by my fears. The train pulling through the station sent the sheets of papers flipping and flying alongside my courage across the platform. The colourful streak of a dress could not break my stare at the horizon before me. All I could do was watch my dreams rattle away until I could no longer see the train. My jaw aching from my clenched teeth, defeated by my cowardice, I turned and started the familiar walk home.

I would have to try again someday, when I found my courage once more. I would have to try again to justify the meaning of my name, *Shaurya — brave, courageous.*

4

SHAURYA

The drum beat on the second hand of the clock in the classroom. I found the discussions on Advanced Auditing a cruel taskmaster to my morale. Unfortunately, I needed the subject and lectures to prep for the final exams. The professor was dragging all of us through the different auditing methods, giving us real-world scenarios, and making us work through them. Gruelling as it was, it was a good exercise. But I was disconnected from the words coming from the mouth of the man in front of the chalkboard. Every move and note I took was mechanical, emotionless.

Chairs screeching against the floor woke me from my trance. Class had finally ended. I was eager to go home, shut myself in a room where I could truly be alone. Riding through the streets, numbers and charts still echoed through my mind. My shoulders felt lighter with each gear shift of the bike under my feet, but the sting of mental exhaustion grew thicker. I was tired, and the thought that the day was still not over pulled me down. The idea of studying alone tripled the burnt, muddled sensation in my head, which was throbbing and begging for sleep. Blinking, trying to keep my eyes open, I realized I had made it home. The buildings, people, cars and fellow bikers were all a blur and forgotten.

Parking the bike and switching off the engine, I continued to sit on my bike, leaning on the handles. I closed my eyes, wondering if anyone would make a fuss if I slept there. The sounds of my neighbour talking hit my ears. I looked up to her veranda and saw that she was talking with a girl I hadn't seen before, but I was far too tired to engage in conversation. The idea of a shower and bed finally won me over and I pulled myself off my bike.

The world around me remained out of focus as I walked up the stairs on automatic. One foot on a step, I sighed with my shoulders slumped. It was agonizing to know I still had to go up the steps, even though I was fine on a physical level. Willing myself, I started the climb; the motivation was the promise of being home and the torture of class temporarily ended.

'Shaurya.' The voice halted my climb.

It was a gentle and warm sound, but I was afraid to turn to my neighbour, Kasturi. Her family lived on the ground floor of the two-floor row house in which my family and I occupied the second floor. My heart fluttered and I gripped the railing tighter. I couldn't decide whether I was blessed or cursed to have such a wonderful girl living next door to me. Her lips curled in the most stunning smile and being near her made people around her happy. I loved how her hair was never worn in the same style, the auburn strands wavy when set loose. She was colourful, bright inside and out, and her words often inspired me.

Her hair was braided today, and she had placed a decorative hair pin in it. Bright and fancy patterns adorned any fabric she wore or carried with her, and the colours were usually a spectrum of orange, purple and green. If you failed to be lost in the overwhelming sensation of happiness she carried, her soft brown eyes would draw in your soul. They were a soft, tender colour, much like the tone in the finest suede in a shop.

Kasturi was a year younger than me, but our outlook on life was so drastically different. I faced the world with a choking amount of fear, especially when it came to my dreams and desires. She was able to face even the ugliness within this world with a smile and lived with no regrets. She loved what she was doing, and was very focused on completing her MBA in Finance. The man from the bench would agree that she followed his philosophy of taking leaps to accomplish one's wants in life. I admired her for that ability — it made me jealous.

As much as I yearned to spend a moment with her, right now, I was still feeling the sting of my cowardice from the railway station.

'Shaurya?' she repeated, her tone shifting to worry. 'Are you feeling okay?'

No words came to mind. My mouth went dry and my thoughts hid from me. My grip on the stairway rail tightened further, my hand aching as a cold sweat made me shudder.

Her hand shook my shoulder, a burst of warmth catching my attention. 'Are you okay, Shaurya?'

Avoiding her eyes, emotionless, I managed to nod a weak reassurance that I was fine.

My eyes hit her lips as she asked again, 'Is something wrong?'

Squeezing my eyes tight, I willed myself to wake up. Coming back to the present, I gave a weak smile and shook my head. I was afraid that if I spoke my lie, she would see through me; a coward. Why did everything frighten me? Indecisiveness haunted me, my heart raged against my mind in even the smallest tasks.

Her hand fell away, the coldness of my fears weaving back across my shoulders.

'Well, I wanted to introduce you to my cousin.' Her hand motioned down the stairs where the girl she'd been talking to waited. 'Miraya, this is the friend and neighbour I was telling you about.'

The pride in her voice when she gave me that title did me no justice. Miraya seemed unmoved by it, but she shifted a little in response. She was taller, and a little stern in her overall appearance. It was hard to read her, her lips neither smiling nor frowning as they came to elegant points at the corners of her mouth. Her eyes were tired, and they shouted that she had experienced more of life than I could ever dare to at this point in my own. Her hair was up in a bun, but a few strands had escaped; the colour deep and dark, only flashing brown in the sunlight. She wore a complimenting, yet simple dress. Hey eyes peered up at me with a judging look.

'Uh, hello Miraya,' I nodded, my eyes too scared to meet even this stranger's own.

She nodded, her face taut and eyes looking me over. It seemed she was unsure of the man she saw before her, but I couldn't blame her for the notion. How could she not be wary of this stranger; even I didn't know what to think of myself. There was nothing special about me at a glance. I was like every other student, brown eyes with black hair styled like a majority of my classmates. Put me in a crowd, and I would be lost in a sea of people, unlike Kasturi.

'Miraya's an amazing interior designer.' She motioned for me to come back down the stairs, but I only took a step down. 'I'm so lucky to have her come all the way here. She's going to help us renovate our home. I can't wait to see what magic she does!'

'Renovations?' I felt obligated to ask.

'Yes! Oh, did I forget to tell you?' Kasturi laughed. 'I have been so busy, I suppose it slipped my mind.'

'I suppose ...' My smile was half-hearted.

'Well, we're making some changes, and Miraya is going to help me design the rooms.' Her eyes narrowed as her cheeks were pushed high with her grin. 'I still can't believe she left Mumbai to come here to help me. She's been fussing over my colour choices, so maybe you can join us for a cup of coffee and be a tie-breaker?'

The word *Mumbai* stung. I bit my tongue, unable to keep the claws of my regret from ripping their way back to the front of my mind. Kasturi's words were pulling away from me. I felt deaf and mute in my emotions, the sun beating down on me adding to the discomfort of it all. The grip of my hand around the rail kept me grounded just enough not to fall forward. My brow furrowed, I was losing my false smile. Could I be this tired from class? No, this was my soul in turmoil, still glued to that bench on Platform No. 2, waiting for me to voice my answer.

'Does that sound okay to you, Shaurya?' Blinking, I found Kasturi's lips again with their faithful smile. 'Or are you busy with studies?'

Shaking the haze from my eyes, I forced a smile. 'Yes, with final exams ... I am exhausted.'

I fell silent again, struggling to move my legs or to

come up with more to say. Kasturi seemed to be the only one in the mood for conversation.

'Oh, I forgot to ask how your mom is doing.' She was still trying to pry a conversation from both her cousin and me. 'Wasn't she sick?'

'She was,' I nodded and I leaned against the stairway railing. 'It was a minor cold. I'll tell her you said hi.'

'I'd love to introduce her to Miraya.' She gave her cousin a nod to join the conversation, but she just shrugged and looked away. 'How was your class today?'

'Exhausting ...' I breathed. 'Full of numbers and reviewing information for audit methods.'

Kasturi twisted her face. 'Yikes, sounds agonizing.'

'You have no idea ...' I glared up at the sky; perhaps I could hide the emotions betraying me this way.

She paused, looking from me to Miraya. Again, we both kept silent.

Placing a hand on her hip, she attempted a conversation again. 'Was the bike ride home okay?'

'I suppose ...' Again I failed to finish the train of thought, and my words trailed off.

'Well, Shaurya,' her tone now reminded me of when my mom used to scold me. 'You look like death warmed over. I should leave you alone to rest. Perhaps you've caught your mom's cold.'

Mumbling under my breath, I said, 'If only I were that lucky.'

'What was that?' Her eyes widened.

'Nothing.'

'Uh …' Miraya's voice drew our eyes back to the bottom of the steps. 'Have you been to Mumbai? You seem familiar …'

I winced. 'No, I have never been to Mumbai.'

'I'm sure I've seen you some place,' Miraya insisted.

My lips tightened. The stinging in my heart couldn't endure any more reminders that I had given up on my dreams, again. Worse, the weight of it was increasing each time I tried and failed to break my chains. Waving at them, I gave an empty smile and started up the stairs. Miraya gave a nod, a smile as unsteady as my own on her face. My exhaustion was dragging me to the front door; I wanted to be alone. In fact, deep down, I felt I deserved to be alone for the cowardice I'd displayed.

Fumbling in my pockets, I found the keys to the front door. Unlocking it, I could hear the gentle murmur of Kasturi and Miraya's voices moving away. Looking back down, I caught Miraya's gaze. She seemed so sure she had seen me before. Perhaps in another life, where I actually made it on the train to Mumbai, it could have been true. An ache tightened in my chest, and I pushed through the door. The click of it closing behind me brought temporary relief. Leaning against it, I felt ready to fall asleep and let that sour day fade away.

5

SHAURYA

Sleep was evading me. Tossing and turning in the dark room was torture. Staring at the ceiling, I could not shake the sorrowful look of the man as he moved away from me. Why was this time so different from all the others? I had been to the railway station multiple times before. It wasn't the first time I had failed to take that life-changing step to board the train; yet, this last time would not fade away. Was I being punished?

My mom opened the door, not realizing I was inside. 'What's wrong? You look drained.'

Furrowing my brow, I shrugged. 'Just feeling down today.'

She set down the basket of clean clothes she was carrying inside my room, her mouth twisting with thought. After a minute or two, hands on her hips, she made the face that indicated she had thought of something. Nodding in agreement to herself, she turned her focus to me and I couldn't help but smile at this silly ritual of hers.

'Why don't you go outside, to the terrace?' Again, she nodded to herself. 'Some fresh air, maybe the sunlight, might brighten your mind some.'

'I might just do that ...' I turned my eyes back to the ceiling and its mundane landscape.

She scoffed as she walked deeper into my room. 'I can't believe you still have this frame up.'

I bit my tongue.

'What does it mean again?' I kept quiet and I could feel her eyes on me before she finally gave up. 'Fine, Shaurya. At least go get some air. I hate seeing you so disheartened.'

Caving, I looked to her. 'I know ...'

She came closer and kissed my forehead, her hands cupping my face. 'You are a wonderful son. I feel blessed to be your mom.'

I forced a smile. 'And I couldn't ask for a more loving mom.'

Content that she had cheered me up, she left the room. Rolling out of bed, I walked to my desk. A stack of textbooks on accounting and financial subjects towered on one side. I rubbed the side of my jaw, in no mood to pick up any of them. Considering the haze I was in, the book from my earlier class seemed the least of all the evils. Never in my life had I felt so drained from thinking. It was now late afternoon, and the sun was hot and bright. I was far from hungry, and I thought perhaps studying for an hour or two would build up the appetite I had been lacking all day.

I followed the building around to the common terrace, a favourite spot of mine for reading. The two-storey walls there made it shady and cool. There was a view of the train tracks as well as the street leading to my CA classes. In the terrace were cluttered groups of potted plants next to planters and chairs. The atmosphere was freeing, and I hoped it would slow the wave of thoughts.

Marching in, I stumbled to a halt. Miraya was there, and she was writing something; but she paused as soon as she saw me. It was a rare treat to not be alone in the terrace, but I was thankful it was someone who wasn't in the mood for conversation. I smiled, my happiness coming across awkwardly to me. Miraya gave a half smile in response and went back to her writing, ignoring my movements. I sat some way off from where she was with her book and pen. This was my way of making it clear that I was here to keep to myself.

Opening my textbook, I flipped through the pages, wondering where I should start. The lecture was a blur in my mind. I wondered if I had even retained anything. My instincts made me look back to Miraya. She had twisted around to look at me with her hazel eyes, her brow furrowed. I froze, unsure of what she might be thinking about me. Her lips parted, but shut quick and firm as she turned back to her book.

Staring at her back, I was confused. To turn to someone not once but twice was strange. Why was she so sure she had seen me before? So much so that she had even thought about asking me once more, I was sure of it.

Watching her for several minutes, flipping pages without glancing at them, I marvelled over her expression. Her eyes were locked on her book, her pen flying with such confident strokes. Whatever words she was laying to paper, she was clearly passionate, feeling them from her heart down her arm, and leaving them there on the pages of her notebook. Pausing between my meaningless page flips, I found myself smiling. It was quite a thing to take in: there was so much more life to the way Miraya was writing versus the masses of students I had watched in my classes. What on earth could she be writing to lose herself so deeply in the pages in her lap?

The sound of a train horn drew my attention away from Miraya and back to my feeling of failure. I watched it going past with a sour look on my face. Why was it so hard to choose a life for myself? Every part of me wanted to start the life I imagined having, living. Instead, I was sitting here on this terrace, and it was no different from the glued sensation the bench had brought me. My jaw ached as I fought back tears of frustration. This was my life, here on this terrace, where I could make my parents proud by finishing my final exams, become a CA. But deep down, this was far from what I wanted to be. ...

Breaking away from the fading noise of the train, I realized Miraya had left. My regrets and hopes were pulling at me so deeply, that I was letting the world move without me. I decided to abandon the heat of the day and went back home.

I could hear my mom in the kitchen, the heat from the stove wafting from the doorway as she buzzed about. Walking in, I skirted around her for a glass of water. She tapped my side, I shifted and she grabbed a pot from the cabinet below. Seeing I was adding to her troubles, I worked my way to the dining room table, where my dad sat, reading the newspaper.

'How's your day going, Shaurya?' he asked, looking over his glasses at me.

'Okay,' I said, sitting and taking another gulp of water.

He lifted an eyebrow, looking back at his papers. 'Are the classes going well for you?'

'Y-yes.'

The paper dropped all the way to the table. 'Is something the matter?'

I opened my mouth, but looking him in the eyes changed what I wanted to say. 'I'm just exhausted. The topic we are covering is filled with a lot of information and it's worn me down.'

Grunting, he folded his hands together. 'Are you sleeping okay? Or are you coming down with something?'

'No …' I shook my head. 'Just tired. A lot of material to cover.'

Scratching his chin, he looked me over. 'Well, if you need anything, Shaurya, don't hesitate to ask.'

'Yes, Dad.' Staring at the water in my glass, I wished I could feel the same transparency with my dad about my dreams. 'I'll be okay … I always pull through.'

Chuckling, he nodded with a wide grin. 'You stun me every time, Shaurya. I am proud of how far you've come. Keep it up.'

I slid out of my chair, my stomach turning. No longer was I hungry or thirsty. My dad meant well, but what would he think if he knew I had been at the train station that morning? What would he say to the idea that I wanted to throw away all my hard work and step on a train with a smile on my face?

6

MIRAYA'S DIARY

For some reason, I felt like writing today. It's been three months since I last sat down to write anything. But I experienced something interesting today. Something so surreal I cannot help but feel it needs to be written down.

Kasturi's neighbour and friend Shaurya is the same guy from the railway station. What are the odds? He was standing motionless, staring at the train as if he wanted to catch it, but something was stopping him. What could it be, I wonder. He didn't even care to help me with my bags or react to my papers flying away. In fact, I don't think he even noticed me or the entire situation. His eyes were so sad before he turned and left me there, struggling to gather my things.

But this whole event has urged me to write. I feel as if I am talking to a friend after years of being apart. I stopped writing for a while because, because within these pages is the fall of everything I adored in life. These pages have witnessed my past. It stings, knowing if I dare go one page back I will feel the stab in my heart and tears will betray me yet again.

Writing here, in you, is something I still miss doing. I've always done so, and after those painful moments, I couldn't will myself to do it. I am glad I have been driven to take my pen to paper. It's not as frightening as I had thought. In fact, I feel like I have regained a piece of myself. Thanks to the odd event in the Jaipur railway station with Shaurya.

And today, on the terrace again, he was giving a train that same look as before. It was as if his beloved was running away from him, leaving him behind to go back home. What or who is waiting for him? I can't help but wonder about it. It all seems so strange. Why do I even care? And here I am writing after so long. Isn't that strange as well? Finding myself fascinated by this stranger … something I vowed would never happen again.

So why am I here in Jaipur? Kasturi is renovating her home, and naturally I have come to lend my talent to my wonderful cousin. I adore Kasturi; she's so warm and loving, and being here with her makes me happy. We're planning out the kitchen at the moment, and then we'll move on to the bedrooms. As always, Kasturi wants bright and vivid colours. Before we do her room, Aunty has made it clear her room is to be next.

I'm super excited about this! I was a little nervous about leaving Mumbai, but there isn't much there for me anymore. My dream to be an interior designer is a reality, and I cannot be more proud of myself. I do miss some of my favourite spots and a few of my friends that I left behind, but then again, I am just a train ride away. Jaipur is a nice change. Here I can relax, not feel like I need to look over my shoulder. In fact, I think this is what I needed, a fresh start to regain the confidence I lost in Mumbai.

Tomorrow we may go looking at some furniture and furnishings to complement the ideas we have. Nothing is more satisfying to see the things I put on paper come to life in a room. Kasturi is so excited by some of the sketches I brought with me. I had worked out a few ideas on the train ride over, but sadly I lost some to the wind when that man slammed into me.

It did give me a chance to draw up new versions with my cousin's input, so I can only be happy with the fact that it worked out for the best. But I am having to wrangle with her colour demands! Some of the combinations she suggests are a little too much, even for me.

I am not so sure how I feel about seeing Shaurya around. It still makes me a little mad how he ignored my plight at the railway station, but then I think about that heartbroken face he carries. He didn't even notice I was standing by him, staring at the train with him.

Anyway, despite it all, I am excited to be here, writing. It feels good, it feels right.

7

SHAURYA

The professor was droning on at the chalkboard, his voice muddled in my ears. Propping my head on my arm, I found my eyes wandering to the windows. Some birds flew past and I gazed at them unseeingly. The sharp sound of the chalk against the board demanded my attention. Clearing his throat, the professor went on, and I failed to comprehend the words thrust upon me.

My mind refused to take in any more for the day. Leaning back in my chair, I rubbed my eyes and tried once more.

'This is going to be your homework today. I expect everyone to finish it for the next class. Be sure to read chapter seven, and take notes. I will not, and I repeat, *not* cover that chapter in detail in class. Instead, we will take the information from your reading and practice a real scenario audit with the method it covers. If you have questions, be sure to have them ready at the start of class.' He looked up at the clock behind him. 'My time's up. Have a blessed day.'

I darted out the door, not wanting to be trapped at my desk for even one second more. It was a gorgeous day, a mild breeze cutting through the heat. Zig-zagging through crowds in the market, I caught a glimpse of a bright orange and yellow patterned skirt familiar to me. Slowing, I sat straighter on my bike, and looked around. Another flash brought me to a stop and I waved. Indeed, I had spotted Kasturi buying something from a shop and I was starving for a chance to regain some of the inspiration she seemed to flood into me. Waving again with my hand held high, I inhaled, readying myself for a loud shout.

'Kasturi!'

She spun around and, when she saw me, she smiled her contagious smile. She waited for me to ride up to her and then said, 'Hi, Shaurya! Are you headed home?'

'Yes, a couple of lectures were cancelled so I was picking up some stationery for an assignment. And you?'

'Same.'

Looking around, I nodded at the café nearby. 'Want to join me for some coffee?'

Her smile widened. 'Of course. I'm glad you seem to be feeling better today. It's been far too long since we sat and chatted.'

'Sorry, I've had a lot on my mind lately.' Parking my

bike, I walked up and held the door open for her. 'This one is on me.'

'Are you sure?' she asked, sitting down at a table, looking at me in surprise.

'It's the least I can do. The usual?'

She nodded in reply.

I returned with our coffees, eager to spend some time alone with Kasturi. 'I didn't mean to come off as rude to your cousin. I just wasn't in a talkative mood.'

'I noticed.' She took a sip. 'But I don't think Miraya was in the mood to talk much either. She had a bad start to her day.'

I slid my chair closer. 'I can't say mine was much better.'

'She plans on staying here for awhile,' she said. She looked a bit pensive then and continued, 'May I ask you to help her out? Make her feel welcome?'

'S-sure.' Sipping my own coffee, I stole a moment to take in her eyes. 'So she's here to help with the renovations in your place, right?'

'Yes!' She gave a toothy smile. 'You should see her sketches, they're wonderful!'

Nodding, I felt as if her presence was lightening the weight of my regrets. 'I can't wait to see them.'

'In fact we finished the designs for the kitchen and we just broke ground to start the work in there.' She sighed, her eyebrows lifting as she stared down into her coffee. 'Until we finish, we'll be eating out a lot.'

'That's not such a bad thing.' It was a rare chance for me to be the positive thinker. 'You can steal the opportunity to go to the movies or do a little more shopping. Get out of the house.'

She laughed. 'Speaking of movies, what did you think of that new action flick that came out last week?'

I took a moment to think of which one she was talking about. 'The recent secret agent one?'

She nodded, drinking her coffee and awaiting my answer, her doe-like eyes on me.

'Well, the storyline fell flat, to be honest.' I leaned back in my chair. 'The stunt work and action scenes were excellent, but I can't believe the plot was practically missing. A movie should tell a good story; any director who fails to put a story in visual format is either lazy or has failed. It was just one epic action moment after another, but I suppose there are people out there who like that sort of film.'

Kasturi smiled, placing her coffee on the table. 'I felt confused and lost in the story, but hearing your insight I realize that was what the problem was — it didn't have a story to follow at all. Shaurya, maybe you should consider going in the field. You always seem so knowledgeable about it —'

My expression halted her words. 'I, I've been thinking about being ... I've been wanting to go after my dreams a lot, lately.'

'I would love to hear what that is, someday.' It was like she had dived into my soul, looking for my hidden dream.

'But it's not so easy to make that decision ...' Pausing, my eyes fell to my coffee, the steam swirling up, wrestling with itself much like my mind and heart. 'My family would prefer that I continue with the CA course.'

She frowned. 'But that's not your dream, is it, Shaurya?'

My chest ached to hear the fact said aloud, and it slammed my ears with unforgiving force. 'I have several dreams, Kasturi. That is only one, and most I cannot do without giving up on the others.'

She nodded. 'It's hard to take that risk, to tie yourself down to only one ambition, but even if you fail, you'll never live a life of regret. Life is forgiving. Every experience, failed or successful, is never wasted. All the time spent does work towards a final goal, some known and some newly-discovered on the journey. You have to have faith in yourself, confidence in who you are and want to be, and be brave enough to take the steps towards achieving your dream.'

'I lack the courage,' I mumbled.

Her hand touched mine, bringing my eyes back to hers as my heart fluttered. 'Shaurya, you lack faith in yourself most of all. Have faith, courage will follow.'

Mustering a smile, I breathed, 'Thank you for the advice, Kasturi ... but tell me,' I said, eager to change the focus of our conversation, 'what of *your* dreams? What do you want out of life?'

Her face blossomed into a huge smile that reached up into her eyes. 'My dreams,' she said, 'there are so many.'

She began to outline her hopes and goals for the future. As she put words to those dreams, I became enraptured by the pure joy, the utter excitement that threaded through her aspirations. I heard letters: MBA. MNC. It was like listening to a beautiful song; the kind that could make you weep with appreciation.

I blinked quickly, realizing that tears were starting to gather in my own eyes at her excitement. Her words were filled with so much confidence, so much optimism. I was proud of her for having such a solid goal and not being afraid to go after it. At the same time, my own frustrations came to the surface again. I took a long sip of my coffee while I brought my emotions back in check.

I lowered my cup and met her eyes once again. She laughed, a little self-consciously. 'They probably sound silly to you, though,' she said.

'No,' I said, shaking my head passionately. 'They are perfect. They reflect you.'

Our eyes locked and held there for a long moment and I could start to see other dreams gathering in hers — dreams she had not given voice to. Could she see me as part of those wistful, secret plans?

I cleared my throat. My eyes fell away from hers as I quickly grasped for a new topic of conversation. 'So, after the kitchen, which room will you renovate next?'

Furrowing her brow, she sighed at the sudden change of topic. 'We are still finishing the final touch-ups on the designs but my mom wants her bedroom to be done next.'

'Where will your mom sleep while her room is being renovated?' I was relieved Kasturi had accepted the change in topic; I aimed to walk away from my hidden ambitions for the time being. 'I doubt she will accept sleeping on the couch.'

She laughed, and the last of the tension broke. 'Far as I was told, if we plan this well, they should be able to do the requested changes in a week. Don't forget she's not shy about telling me and Miraya to sleep on the couch while she claims my bed or the guestroom.'

Smiling, I finished the last of my coffee. 'Well, Kasturi, I must get going. I have homework to do for tomorrow's class. You know how revisions can be. Do you need a ride home?'

She shook her head. 'I still have some work to do around here. You take care, Shaurya,' she said, her smile warm. 'Thank you for the coffee, and we should get back in the habit of talking like this more often.'

I nodded with a smile. Dodging out the café door, I felt relieved to have ended the conversation before she had a chance to circle back to prying into my dreams. Despite the pressure, I was happy to get some words of encouragement. I needed the armour she gave me to face the inner conflicts needling me. Deep down, I was standing in my own way, but without decisiveness, I had no weapon to strike down the obstacles in my mind.

8

Miraya's Diary

I had a wonderful phone conversation with my parents today. I miss them so much, but they are happy and healthy so I am satisfied with that.

Of course, they wanted to know how I am after … after. I don't even like to talk about that time in my life. I'm not ready to think about it.

So I held a smile in my voice and I told them that I was fine.

Fine. It's amazing how such a small word can portray such an important state of mind.

I guess I am fine, though. In fact, as I told my parents this on the phone, I was happy to realize that it really was true. I told them of my journey to Jaipur and how much fun it is to be with Kasturi again. Even though I am here to work, being with her gentle spirit reminds me of when we were kids. And I find that I am content once more. At least, I am much more content here than I was before.

I wonder about Shaurya, though. He is a man who is far

from fine or content. It's not really my business, nor do I want to make it my business ... but I am so curious about the sadness that envelops him, like a cold breeze slipping under your warmest scarf.

9

ANUBHAV

Bangalore

I completed my MBA with high marks. Confident with my education and determination pushing me forward, I launched my tech startup in six months.

I climbed to the top quickly, and those who worked with me were amazed at how rapidly the business took off.

We celebrated our success one evening after the quarterly results showed that we were still in a high-growth period. My company was heading for record numbers and a glorious future. I couldn't wait to show my parents what I had built; my palace, of sorts.

In a way, I felt like a king at the table that night.

'Let's raise our glasses to Anubhav!' one of my colleagues stood up and said, his cheeks red with alcohol. 'To his ingenious concept! And to his hunger for success! Thank you, Anubhav, for letting us join you on this amazing journey!'

A great roar of whistles, compliments, and clicking of glasses ran through the restaurant. We all drank from our glasses, and laughter ensued as everyone made it a point to pat me on the back.

'Anubhav, you have a natural talent as a businessman!' My colleague who had given the toast had worked his way to me from across the table. 'You taught me so much during our time in college, and to see it in action, I am humbled.'

Laughing, I shook my head. 'I've been picturing this day since I was a child, believe it or not.'

'Incredible! What a feeling it must be to achieve one's dream!'

Everyone's faces were a blur, nothing but the smiles clear in my eyes. Raising my glass, I caught the attention of everyone at the table. 'Silicon Valley, here we come!'

There was a roar and more clinking of glasses. 'To Silicon Valley!'

In the six months after that, it hit big, real big. I found myself making major deals, meeting with the bigwigs in the industry, and making a name for myself. Before my eyes, my dream, my business, was growing aggressively. I felt I had everything I could ever hope for, and had made my parents proud.

I was thinking of just how happy my parents would

be as I sat in a meeting one late monsoon evening. It was raining, and I was grateful it wasn't a more severe downpour. My parents, tired of waiting for me to come home, were en route to meet me after a long time.

My phone vibrated on the conference table and I pushed the button to stop it. It was the third time in the last ten minutes or so. The number was unknown and only one voicemail had been left. I didn't want to interrupt the meeting as we were deep in discussion about the chance to expand one line of products by partnering with a new and upcoming business. Again, the phone buzzed and the display flashed *Unknown*.

'Do you need to take that, Mr. Anubhav?' My cheeks turned red that the meeting had halted because of me. Before I could answer, he continued, 'In fact, let's take a fifteen-minute break.'

As I walked out of the conference room the phone vibrated in my hand again. Angry, I answered it.

'This better be important!' I stepped out into the hallway and began pacing back and forth.

'I-is this Mr. Anubhav?' The timid voice caught me off-guard and I stopped pacing.

'Yes.' As I answered, I asked myself, *Why is my heart racing?*

10

SHAURYA

Jaipur

The traffic didn't fight me as hard on the ride home from the café. Kasturi's words of encouragement were still echoing through me, caressing my soul, whispering, *have faith in yourself.* She was a special kind of friend who made me feel like nothing was out of my reach; that I could achieve anything. A life without her, without her glances and smiles, would be insignificant and barren. The warmth of her smile led me through the sourest of thoughts. At times it felt like I was standing in a rainstorm of doubts and a beam of sunlight had brought me back to life. Kasturi was indeed special to me.

My shoulders were lighter and I was eager to contemplate my dreams once more. Kasturi was right. My courage suffered because of a lack of confidence and faith in myself. These alone were more than enough to tie me down to the bench.

Finally home, I was eager to lose myself in my thoughts in the comfort of the terrace. I slowed down when I hit the threshold of the terrace as I saw Miraya glancing up from her reading for a second. Her cheeks flushed, and she shut what looked to be a journal or diary of sorts. The motion was too abrupt and it slipped from her hand. It fell on the terrace floor, and the pages flew open. She scrambled to pick it up, a sense of guilt in her motions. It was as if I had caught her red-handed in a crime and spooked her mid-act.

'Woah …' I blinked. Hands raised to show I was no threat, I took a few steps closer to her. 'Relax, I didn't mean to startle you, Miraya.'

She looked up at me, wide-eyed and hugging her diary. 'Stay away from me.'

The hiss in her voice stung. 'Miraya?'

She darted out of the terrace and down the stairs leaving me completely confused. Chasing after her, I stopped at the top of the stairs and called after her.

'Miraya!' I couldn't see her anywhere; she had been too fast.

Running my hand through my hair, I walked back to the terrace, baffled. Had I done something wrong? If so, what was it? Perhaps I came off as rude the other day on the terrace, by not talking to her. She did seem certain she knew me.

Sitting down, I closed my eyes, trying to recall if I had seen her before. Instead, my mind took me back to papers falling and the man's frown at the railway station. Why did those memories come back into my mind so easily?

Dropping my bag to the ground, I leaned on my knees as my mind spiralled in circles. The look on Miraya's face was haunting me. She had run off so fearfully; and the stiffness in her body as I took those steps closer to her made me feel like a monster. What exactly was in that book? And what did it have to do with me?

This was my third time meeting her. Each time she had acted so strangely. What was it with me that brought this out in her? Regardless, I couldn't help but worry if she was okay. I would have to ask Kasturi about it, maybe she could tell me something about Miraya's behaviour. For some reason, deep down, I felt an agonizing guilt. Flustered, I gave up trying to enjoy the terrace and shuffled back home. The door shut heavily behind me, and before I made it through my own door, my dad called out to me.

'Come, sit down and talk with me for a minute.' He was sitting in the living room enjoying some iced tea. 'How are your classes going?' he asked.

I shrugged. I hated talking about how well my studies were going; as much as I excelled, my heart was still not in it. 'Good, I guess,' I mumbled.

'Just good? Come on,' he teased. 'I bet you're doing a fantastic job.'

'Yes, I guess you could say that,' I admitted.

He leaned forward and clasped me on the shoulder. 'See? I knew this was where you were meant to be.'

'But —'

'No, Shaurya. You are excelling, just like I knew you would. I'm proud of you, son. I was telling everyone in my office about you and they ask all the time. It makes me so proud to tell them what a great success you are in your studies and how perfect you will be as a CA.'

I winced. As much as I wanted to enjoy his pride, I resented the fact that it was pride in the dream he chose for me, not one I'd chosen for myself.

Seeing my discomfort, he quickly changed the subject. 'Did the class run late today?'

'No,' I said, sitting across from him. 'I ran into Kasturi in the market.'

'Oh?' This piqued his interest and he smiled. 'How is Kasturi doing?'

Blushing, my eyes fell away from his face. 'She's good.'

'Did you talk for long?' He took a sip of his drink, waiting for my reply with a sparkle in his eye.

Desperate to avoid the goofy expression on his face, I looked to the ceiling. 'I asked her to join me for a coffee. And we did talk for some time at the café.'

'Good, good,' he nodded happily. 'Didn't her cousin come from Mumbai recently?'

'Yes, Miraya is her name and she's apparently a famous interior designer,' I said, and continued before he could ask any more questions, 'I'm going to go do some studying in my room. Call me when dinner is ready.'

My room was dark, but this was typical, this late in the evening. The sun had reached the other side of the building, casting shade across the outer wall. Sitting on my bed, I grabbed one of my photography magazines. My eyes fell on my camera, which I now rarely used. It pained me to see it, a relic of a life I had once dared to dream about. Flopping onto my back, I flipped from one random page to the next. Images and colours flashed before me: people, animals, flowers, sprawling landscapes and skilfully-altered imagery blinked in and out of existence.

Tiring of the taunts of what could have been, I placed the magazine on my nightstand. None of these distractions had taken my mind off Miraya's face. What could warrant such a volatile reaction? Was she more angry than fearful? Even then, what had brought it on? I ruffled my hair in frustration. All I wanted was to make a good impression on her for Kasturi's sake. I had failed, somewhere and somehow. My life seemed to be spiralling in all directions, and I couldn't tell which part I needed to clean up first. At least my parents were content with me.

11

Miraya's Diary

I felt like a kid again, caught doing something bad. My heart is still racing. He came out of nowhere, scaring me half to death. It was as if he knew what I was feeling. I thought of him and he manifested, making my innermost feelings naked. AHH! I was so scared I dropped you, Diary! In fact, I think I literally threw you to the ground in the heat of the moment!

Oh, and when he came closer! I thought my heart would burst from my chest! I was so scared! Being near him, it was frightening.

This was not the heartless man from the platform. He seemed happier today; seeing him now versus when he ignored me at the railway station feels so drastically different. He seemed soulless then. I wonder if he even realizes his friend slammed into me. How could he not, when my papers and drawings were flying past his feet?

But here, he seems like a different person, and it scares me. What could make someone act like that and not even recall a moment so bizarre? Shaurya is a baffling man ... maybe I should rethink my actions ... I don't know what to do.

Part of this reminded me of my past. Perhaps that's where the fear came from, and worse, the irrational reaction. Shaurya isn't ... well he hasn't exactly been hurtful to me. I can't be mad at a person who can't even remember what happened. Still, something about him brings up old wounds and ... and I can't stand it. I came here to wash away those feelings, yet they rear their ugly head every time I see Shaurya. It frightens me to even be close to someone again, and maybe I fear becoming friends with Shaurya.

12

Miraya's Diary

Today was an interesting day. Aunty asked me to go to Shaurya's place. His mom has wallpaper in her room that Aunty loves and would like to have in her own bedroom after the renovation.

I'd met Shaurya's mom once before when she came over to visit to see the work done so far, but I was still a little scared to go alone, to be honest. However, Shaurya's mom is so sweet and gentle. I was happy to see Shaurya wasn't home. The wallpaper in her room was interesting. I made sure to sketch it out since I hadn't seen that pattern before, not even in the large stores back in Mumbai. When I told her I was done, she insisted I look at the wallpaper in Shaurya's bedroom. She wouldn't take no for an answer, and anyway Aunty had made it clear that if I could take a look at all the rooms, I should bring some sketches back to her.

Shaurya's room wasn't what I expected. I would have imagined it to be more reflective of someone studious, with stacks of books everywhere and motivational posters all over his walls. Instead, I found nothing more than an organized bookshelf and a single empty frame on the wall. Besides that, I was surprised to see photography magazines, CDs, and a camera by his bed.

I asked his mom what the empty frame signified. She smiled, saying Shaurya wanted to take some course in photography or movie-making a few years ago. She said she couldn't remember the exact word for what it was he wanted to do, but he had wanted to go to Mumbai. She and his father hadn't agreed with the idea so the plan had been dropped.

She said, 'It's been a long time now since he gave up on the idea. I don't even know why he has this empty frame on his wall. He never answers me when I ask.'

I suddenly thought of Shaurya's look when he was at the railway station. Was this why he was watching the train to Mumbai in that strange way? He seemed so broken standing there. I suppose I should ask Kasturi, or even Shaurya himself about it.

And the way I acted the last time I saw him, telling him to stay away … I was wrong. I should get to know him better before I judge him so harshly. It's not fair to assume my problems are far greater than his.

13

SHAURYA

March was in full stride, the sun warm, the wind still cool — the perfect time to soak up any outdoor time before summer's flames broiled into life. Enjoying the walk home, I slowed down at the sound of hammers and drilling. I was about to pass Kasturi's place, but Miraya was sitting out on the front steps. She was talking to one of the contractors, sketches and pencils scattered across the stoop next to her. Taking a deep breath, I aimed to walk past without acknowledging her. The hiss of her words was still in my mind, *Stay away from me.*

'Can you get the tiles in that colour?' Miraya's voice reached my ears as I drew closer. 'And if possible some accent pieces to imitate this sketch?'

'I think we can,' nodded the man in the hard hat. 'I'll bring some samples with me tomorrow. We still have to finish the demolition of the old tiles and prep it for laying the new ones.'

'Perfect.' The man left and Miraya's eyes fell on me. 'Shaurya!'

I flinched, turning slowly to face her. 'Hey …'

'I'm sorry for the other day,' she sighed, her eyes darting to the ground as her cheeks flushed. 'The way I acted, I don't know what came over me. I just, well, I was, I am sorry.'

'It's all right.' I could tell from her voice she was hiding something from me, but I mustered a smile to ease her discomfort. 'I didn't mean to startle you. It's not every day I come running into the terrace like that. It's a new place and, well, a man rushing towards you would be frightening, I suppose.'

Her voice lowered, 'Thank you.'

Wanting to shift the awkward mood, I looked beyond her to the open door where workers were going in and out. 'So, how's the work going?'

Her eyes met mine and she peered over her shoulder. 'Pretty good.'

'Kasturi said your art is amazing.' I stopped myself from stepping closer, in fear of repeating what had happened the last time. 'May I see what you're working on?'

'Uh, yes.' She motioned for me to come closer and I sighed in relief. 'Here, this is what I am working on right now.'

'Oh! Still working on the kitchen?' I asked, marvelling over the skill with which images had been drawn across the pages.

'Yes, we picked out counters and appliances, but now I need to figure out the tile-work for the backsplash.' She pointed to a page filled with mock tile patterns and various combinations. 'See, these were some of the ones Aunty, Kasturi, and I were thinking about.'

'I like this one.' I pointed to a blue and white design with accent pieces reminiscent of my mom's Willow Pattern China. 'The accent pieces are a nice touch of the old.'

'That's what Kasturi was thinking.' I couldn't stop the heat rising in my cheeks at being in tune with Kasturi's own likes. 'In fact, she loves drinking tea, and if we can find something like some of her teapots and cups, it would make for a nice touch.'

'I can't wait to see this when it's done.' I smiled, happy that we were both relaxed now. 'Your artwork is nice, Miraya. Even though these are technical in the way you lay them out, the strokes on top of that are very organic and pleasing. You should frame these afterwards as a memento to them coming to life.'

'I might do that,' she laughed. 'But Kasturi may snatch them up and put them in an album with before and after pictures.'

'Very true.' Sensing that the conversation was ending, I decided to leave on a good note. 'Well, Miraya, I need to head home and study. I'll probably see you on the terrace at some point.'

Nodding, she waved, 'Take care, Shaurya.'

14

ANUBHAV

Bangalore

The voice over the phone felt shallow and disconnected.

'Mr. Anubhav, this is Inspector Shiv. I regret to inform you that your parents are ... dead.' The person at the other end waited respectfully for me to say something. Hearing my gasp, he continued. 'They were in a car accident near Bangalore City Railway Station. We have to wait for the official investigation, but right now, it looks like the tyres of their vehicle skid because of the rain and their car rammed into a speeding truck. By the time the ambulance arrived, they had both passed on ...'

'No ...' I gasped. 'This, this can't be ... Where are my parents? I am coming ...'

'I'm sorry for your loss.' He waited for me to catch my breath before continuing. 'The bodies have been taken for the post-mortem now, and you can take them for the funeral tomorrow morning.'

The word *bodies* pierced my heart. I thought back to our last conversation. My parents had been asking me to come home for years, for my birthday, for holidays.

'Just a quick trip home,' my mom had said, over and over. I could picture her wringing her hands while my dad grumbled in the background to leave me alone.

Then he would take the phone from her. I would hear him muttering to her, 'Leave him alone — he'll come back when he can.' And then he would clear his throat as though wiping away any trace of sadness he felt at my not coming home.

And he would tell me how proud he was of me. 'Keep working hard. Keep following your dreams, son. Your mom and I can come visit you when we're able to get away.'

Finally, they were coming to see me. I didn't go to them; I made them come to me. And now they were gone.

I grabbed my chest, struggling to breathe. 'I asked them to come here, and I sent them to their graves! I should have cancelled the meeting. I should have gone to pick them up at the station instead of sending a cab.'

'Mr. Anubhav,' the voice struggled to capture my dissolving attention, 'it was an accident. No one could have —'

My knees buckled. I dropped my phone. The reality

that I was alone, completely alone, rattled through my soul as I sank to the floor.

They were supposed to be joining me for dinner. I invited them to Bangalore, and they had promised, so there wasn't much fuss about me going to Jaipur. If I had gone to them. …

Over and over, I played it in my mind. If I had gone, it could be me dead instead of them. It should have been me! They had each other, whereas I was alone. No other family to turn to and no one to hold my hand or a shoulder to cry on. I felt the sting of reality stabbing my soul.

My dream had consumed me, denied me the desire to pursue a life with another person, or even friends.

I'm not sure when or how, but reality quickly dissolved into some strange, twisted state of existence. Why hadn't I dropped everything to go home? What was there for me anymore?

I didn't eat or sleep. I only wanted to make the pain go away. In lonely desperation, I looked for answers in a bottle of whiskey.

I heard my dad's words again and again as I wandered the streets, pain and numbness warring in my heart. 'I'm proud of you, son.'

~

My colleagues arranged for the funeral the next day and I found myself in front of the bodies of my parents for the final rituals.

I barely remember stumbling at the cemetery, but suddenly I was aware of the shadows around me. The alcohol bottle in my pocket hit the pavement with a dull clunk and reminded me of my broken heart. The noise caught the attention of the priest, who hurried toward me.

'Anubhav, you're drunk,' he whispered, trying to get me to look him in the eyes. 'This is no way to honour the lives of your parents …'

Drunk and angry, I shoved his hand off my shoulder. How dare he try to tell me how to live my life when I should have ended up in the ditch, somewhere between Bangalore and Jaipur. 'Their death is my fault!'

Sighing, the priest grabbed me by my shoulders. 'It was not your fault. Destiny took them when it saw fit. As with everyone, losing both parents is hard. You have been given a heavy burden. Please, Anubhav. Sit, be calm.'

I railed at his sympathetic gestures. 'You don't know what it feels like to be me!' Again, I tried to shove his hands from me, but the world tilted and I fell to the ground. 'If I hadn't asked!'

'I'm sorry, Anubhav.' In my glassy view, I took in that he was motioning for my colleagues. 'For your sake and theirs, I will not let you continue to disgrace yourself here.'

Two of my colleagues hooked an arm each, dragged me outside the cemetery and dropped me home. I sobbed uncontrollably ... something that became a new daily routine for me.

My life after that was a series of blinks; I only opened my eyes long enough to make sure I had made it to a bar or to a bottle to wash away my despair. The funeral was a drunken blur, the rituals a mirage, and my life a distant dream. I had spent my whole life up to this point wanting to make my parents proud of me, only to shame them in their death. The priest's words haunted me. How shamefully I had acted there, in that state.

15

SHAURYA

Jaipur

Over two weeks had gone by since the last time I went to the movies. Up until this point, Friday was a weekly ritual to see the new big release or something comparable. Pacing my room, I looked at the empty frame on my wall. *I should see if Kasturi would like to go,* I thought. *We had such a great conversation at the café. And we seem to have similar taste in movies.* Nodding to myself, I grabbed my phone and dialled her number without hesitation.

'Hello?' I said, overcome with happiness that she had answered. 'Kasturi, it's Shaurya.' My heart raced with excitement. 'You want to go to the movies? Uh, Miraya can come along as well if she wants. I suppose she hasn't been out much since she's been here.'

'Oh, absolutely!' I could feel Kasturi's smile through

her voice. 'Let me ask Miraya if she wants to come. She's been working non-stop, so this is a good chance for her to take a break.'

'Just let me know, okay?' My grin was wide. 'Send a text and I'll book the tickets.'

'All right, I'll message you when I get her answer.'

Hanging up, I lay back on my bed, flipping through a magazine I had bought a couple of days back. This one featured only black-and-white photography. I loved how, despite the lack of colour, the photographers still managed to capture emotion and nuances. Models' eyes still dug deep into your soul with lighting techniques that were able to capture moods and atmosphere. Glancing at my camera, I sighed in frustration. I hadn't touched it in a while.

My phone chirped and danced on my nightstand. It was Kasturi! It was set; I would be booking three tickets. I texted back, smiling wide, as I let her know the time and place. She replied as quickly as I had, asking if I would meet them in front of the theatre as they planned to come directly from a shopping mall. Excited, I grabbed my wallet and keys and headed out.

We all made it there on time and Miraya seemed to be feeling better. At least she didn't seem to be acting weird any more. The lights were dimming as we took our seats, the room darkening as the audience fell silent. As the title sequence started, I let myself be absorbed in the images in front of me. Throughout the film, I could hear Kasturi and Miraya murmuring beside me, chitchatting too low for it to drown out the movie's own sounds. Regardless, it didn't bother me and Kasturi knew I loved movies to the point that I never carried on a conversation during one. If it had anything to do with me, she would ask after the movie was over.

Like coming up to the surface for air, the lights came on in the room and the audience all vibrated with movement once more. Stretching my arms up, I felt like I had gotten back a little piece of myself. Two weeks was far too long between movies.

'That was fantastic!' I looked to them, wondering if they felt the same.

'Yes!' Kasturi stood and then held her stomach with a grimace. 'But I'm starving! Can we go grab a bite to eat?'

Laughing, I nodded. 'Absolutely.'

We made our way to a restaurant and sat down. As we waited for our order to come, I brought up the movie, sharing my favourite moments with them. My heart sang with each wave of laughter I pulled from Kasturi. Even Miraya seemed like a different person. All the unexplained tension I had encountered before seemed to be nowhere in sight. The waiter brought our food and Miraya and I giggled at the speed with which Kasturi pounced on her meal. She almost ran the risk of burning her tongue with a hot spoonful. Another wave of laughter erupted at the table, but was cut short by Kasturi's phone. Her brow furrowed as she answered. We remained silent, waiting for the call to end.

'Sorry guys,' she sighed, ending the call. 'Looks like I need to head to college; there's an important lecture I can't miss. Shaurya, can you drop Miraya off at home after lunch?'

I looked at Miraya and then Kasturi. 'Oh, okay.'

Miraya's tension had come back to her in a flash. 'You can drop me off on your way to lectures, Kasturi. I'll take my lunch to go.'

'Darling, my college is in the other direction from home. By the time I drop you off and double-back, I'll be late.' She lifted an eyebrow. 'Very late.'

'O-okay …' Miraya swallowed, shifting in her seat and tugging on her shirt hem.

A long pause settled over the table, with Miraya and me picking at our food, unsure what to say. Kasturi was rushing to finish her meal, standing as she took in the last few bites. I gave Kasturi an unsteady smile and nod, hoping to reassure her I would take care of her cousin in her absence. She smiled, pushing in her chair.

'I'll catch up with you both later,' Kasturi said, waving as she rushed out the door.

'This is your first time in Jaipur, right Miraya?' I was trying to break the silence, eager to initiate a conversation.

'Yes …' she mumbled.

'Well, we should explore the city then!' I smiled. 'Jaipur holds many stories; you may find some artistic inspiration within its beauty.'

Her eyes came back to me. 'Hmmm … maybe you have a point …'

'If you don't want to go with me, you can always ask Kasturi to take some time off and show you some of the sights.' I didn't want her to feel forced to be with me any longer than she wanted. 'But, if you want to check some out, I am more than happy to show them to you. It will also allow us to spend some time together and get know each other better.'

'Hmmm.' She didn't seem interested.

'You know what, Miraya? You are strange but very interesting.' I thought this would evoke a positive reaction.

'All right, enough.' Her tone was sharp, her eyes digging into me. 'I don't want to talk any more. Stop trying to impress me.'

'Wait, Miraya.' Her response shook me; I couldn't let this go on any longer. 'Listen to me, Miraya.'

'I don't want to hear another word.' Miraya's face was flushed, her eyes angry from something I still didn't grasp. 'I can manage going home by myself.'

Her chair squeaked as she pushed it back; my body jolted and I grabbed her hand. 'Miraya?'

Biting her bottom lip, she pulled her hand back and I let go.

Before she could take another step away, before I failed Kasturi, I pleaded, 'I wasn't trying to impress you or flirt with you. Look, Kasturi asked me to watch over you. She wanted me to help you feel welcome in Jaipur and comfortable while you are here. Miraya, believe me, I was just trying to be a friend. I just, I couldn't even think about flirting with you when I … I like … I like …'

'You like what? Who?' I had her attention; her eyes were boring into me.

Returning the look with a stern stare of my own, I willed my confession to leave my tongue. 'Because, I like Kasturi.'

'W-what?' she blinked, turning her body back towards the table. 'You like Kasturi?'

'Yes,' I sighed, feeling defeated. 'Please don't tell her. Please, not a word to her about me liking her.'

'Y-you're serious? Oh my God!' She sat back down, her face shifting from tense to a playful smirk of disbelief. 'Have you told her?'

'No!'

'What are you waiting for? Tell her how you feel, Shaurya!'

'No way. I couldn't.' I rubbed the side of my jaw. 'If I tried, I don't think I could talk. Please, Miraya, don't tell her.'

'I won't say a word.' She tapped her fingers on the table, mulling over her own thoughts. 'What else are you not saying? Something important that needs to be voiced? At least you can tell me, get it off your chest …'

'Perhaps another day.' I picked at my food, trying to dodge her newfound interest. 'I've got my own lectures soon actually, let me drop you off at home.'

She twisted her lips, lifting an eyebrow in response to the wall I was putting in place.

Catching her expression, I said, 'That is, if you're comfortable with that?'

She laughed, the last of her own wall falling. 'Yes, let's go!'

I remained quiet during the trip home. Watching her close the front door behind her, I sighed. A wave of relief washed over me. If she found out I had lied about having class, I would have lost the trust I managed to build with one quick confession. Walking home, my heart fluttered as my voice echoed in my ears. What had been spoken softly had come across my own ears and mind in a scream. I had voiced the words, and now, the fact that I liked Kasturi had become tangible for the first time.

But my courage fell away quickly, and I strapped my armour back on to hide the secrets in my soul.

16

MIRAYA'S DIARY

I was so mean to Shaurya. Rude, embarrassingly rude. I assumed he was flirting with me, but I was way off base. The honeyed words weren't meant in the manner I had thought them to be. Kasturi had asked him to welcome me here, make me feel comfortable, and Shaurya will do anything to fulfil his promise to her. I have my reasons for being quick to judge, but I never saw this coming ...

Shaurya likes Kasturi.

I wonder if he's ever talked to her about his dream? Does she know about the empty picture frame in his room? That his mom and dad discouraged his ambitions? Does she know that he sits there in the railway station, wanting to leave Jaipur?

I have so many questions for him, so much I want to discover, but he wants to keep it hidden. Maybe my sudden change from foe to friend was too startling. I mean, looking back over those few minutes in the café, after Kasturi left, I was harsh and then prying. But who could blame me? After all, I've been through so much ...

I can tell 'classes' were his way of dodging answering anything about himself. He had offered to take me out on a tour of the city only a minute before. I can't help but be interested in this hidden world of his, especially being aware of how much he adores Kasturi. Next time … next time I will confront him about it all; the railway station, the picture frame, his dreams and his love for Kasturi.

I had a conversation with Kasturi the other day. I asked her how she felt about Shaurya, being careful not to betray his confidence.

Watching carefully, I saw the whisper of hope cross her eyes, before the practical side of her hardened her brow.

'I do like him,' she told me, her words slow to come. 'But I cannot tell him.'

'Why?' I asked my cousin.

She smiled sadly. 'First, I do not know how he feels. We are friends and sometimes our eyes meet and I feel a fire kindling between us. But then he looks away and that flame is doused.'

'You could ask him,' I suggested. 'Or tell him how you feel. Honesty is important.'

Kasturi shook her head. 'I don't know if he is ready for that much honesty. I don't know his whole story, but I sense confusion in his heart. I don't know if it's because of me or other complications in his life.'

I pulled her in for a hug while tears started to streak down her face. 'I never want to hurt him,' Kasturi said. 'I am afraid that if I complicate his story by telling him how I feel, it might bring more pain to his life.'

I thought about what Shaurya had told me and I knew

her words would be a balm to his heart. But she also did have a point — if she told him what was locked in her heart, would it help him or hurt him?

17

SHAURYA

Like the creature of habit I tend to be, I ventured to the terrace. I wish I could say I was surprised about Miraya sitting there, waiting for me, but I knew she had taken a sudden interest in me after I revealed I liked Kasturi. In fact, as I slowed my steps, she stood up to greet me. She motioned for me to sit next to her and I shook my head, waving a hand to say *no thank you*.

'I need some answers from you, Shaurya,' she started.

Goosebumps rose on my skin. 'Go on, ask away.'

'What were you doing at the railway station that day?' Her voice gripped my soul, shaking it with her words. 'I saw you at the station here.'

'When?' My eyes broke from hers, searching the ground for anything less threatening. 'It's been so long since I last went to the station …'

'Lying isn't going to help this time. I know it was you, Shaurya.' Her eyes were burning into me with each revelation. 'You're hiding a lot; your feelings for Kasturi, the camera and magazines in your room, and even the empty picture frame on the wall. I want to know everything. Why are you keeping so much hidden and left in the dark?'

I gnawed at the inside of my cheek, my eyes darting from left to right across the ground. My mouth opened, but she spoke up once more.

'I know I have no right to make this demand of you. I'm sorry, Shaurya.' The tone of her voice softened and I met her eyes again. 'Please know you have no obligation to answer me. I understand if you remain silent.'

With a deep sigh, I said, 'It's all right. We are friends. I mean, considering everything, you have the right to ask me.'

Her lips tightened, anticipating my response for better or worse.

I started slow, my emotions unsure if I was angry or too frightened to miss this chance to voice my dreams aloud for once. 'I have always dreamed about being a filmmaker. Never did I want to be a CA. And the railway station? I went there to catch the train to Mumbai, but in the end, I lacked the courage to take even a step towards it. It wasn't the first time I've been there. I've gone many times, failing each time, unable to leave my parents behind.'

'You should talk to your parents, then.' She was trying to be encouraging. 'They will understand.'

Looking away, I shut my eyes tight as if in pain from some invisible stab wound. 'I wish they would ...'

'Ha-have you tried?' She blinked. 'Have you tried explaining it to them?'

'Once …' I sighed, the sour memory coming to life again.

~

'… and I realized that my parents never fought for their own dreams,' I ended. I had told her about the moment I confessed my desires to my parents. 'The empty frame on the wall? I put that there after I realized that fact so I wouldn't forget this life I live now is my destiny. To be happy with the empty life I will live because I have no luck, as my dad made clear to me.'

'No, Shaurya.' Miraya's fingers tugged on my sleeve, bringing my eyes to hers. '*Anyone* can follow their dream. I'm proof of that …'

I moved my arm so her hold on me was released. 'I need to go …'

My ears were burning and my heart was breaking. It was a heavy burden to hear myself speak about my hidden desires. She respected them; in fact, what little she did say was encouraging, but I was stuck. My courage mortally wounded by my dad's own words and my soul left burnt by my mom's lack of belief and support. Why were the only encouraging words falling from the mouths of Kasturi, and now, even Miraya?

18

MIRAYA'S DIARY

I learned a lot about Shaurya today. I waited for him on the terrace, knowing he would come there at some point. Granted, I cornered him, but I wanted answers. Why were you at the railway station? I asked. He tried to dodge it, but I didn't back down. I like to think I gave him enough respect with my choice of words to let him know I felt he needed to say something, reveal those hidden things about himself.

Shaurya has dreamed of going to Mumbai to become a filmmaker. Several times, he's gone to the railway station, trying to work up the courage to run away. That was why he was there that day.

I asked if he had talked to his parents … and the story was bitter even to my ears. They lack confidence and they want him to follow the same path they have chosen. I did my best to tell him he can do anything, despite what his parents may think of him and his dream. It hurts knowing the empty picture frame on the wall is a reminder to himself that he is living an empty life on this path.

Shaurya is an interesting guy and I am happy to have met him. Destiny is a funny thing and I can't help but feel I am here to help him realize his dream. My dream was to be an interior designer. I fought hard to become what I am today, and now I have plenty of work no matter where I go. Shaurya can do the same, but he just needs to find his courage again.

Despite it all, I am feeling much better since I've been in Jaipur. Now that I know more about Shaurya, and understand the struggles he is facing, I can breathe easier. Here I feel like I can rise above the skeletons in my own closet and help the lives around me to become richer. I think I have finally escaped the weight of my past, though the scars are still there.

19

ANUBHAV

Bangalore

'Anubhav ...' I cringed, recognizing any statement starting with my name and in that tone would be followed by another slice into my heart. 'You've forced our hand.'

I lifted my head from my desk, drool caking my face, and I downed the last sip of whiskey from the bottle in my hand. 'Forced it to do what?'

'We all hated to have to do this ...' His eyes fell away and I sat up in my chair. 'You were the reason we made it this far, but now ...'

'Are you ...' My face wrinkled in pain. 'Are you cutting me out?'

The eyes came back to mine, the heart-wrenching expression on my colleague's face slicing through me. 'We keep hoping you'll get help, sober up, even try to distance yourself or go on an extended leave. Instead, you show up here, barely able to stand, and spend your days drinking and napping in your cabin. It looks bad for the company, especially, to leave you as someone *in charge*.'

I opened my mouth, but then looked at the empty bottle with disdain. 'So this is it. I'm out for good.'

'I'm so sorry, Anubhav ...' He watched as I stumbled to my feet, staggering towards the door where he stood. 'I didn't want to hit you when you were so low, but you're costing the company clients, money.'

I reached the doorknob, just behind him. 'If it were me, I would have tossed myself to the streets long before now ...'

'I hope you find salvation soon, Anubhav.' A tear rolled down his cheek. 'You're a good man; you can do better than this ...'

Who could blame them? I was running the company's image to the ground, and worse, the reputation I had developed as a drunken lost soul could be seen smeared across my face. They cut me out before I could do the same to the business name, and if I were them, I wouldn't have waited as long as they had done with me. I wish I could say I wasn't aware of the damaging, self-destructive habits I'd started, but I would be lying.

20

SHAURYA

Jaipur

Laughter woke me from my daze as I walked down the front path. Kasturi and Miraya were sitting on the stoop looking over some drawings. I paused, knowing I had avoided Miraya since the day I confessed my painful secret. I swallowed my fear; I couldn't miss a chance to talk to Kasturi.

'Hi, girls!' I walked up, smiling. 'What are you two working on?'

Miraya grinned, happy to see she hadn't discouraged me from approaching. 'We are checking on the best options for Kasturi's room.'

'Oh, great!' I was excited to join a conversation where I could show how much I knew about Kasturi's likes and dislikes. 'Well, be sure to leave room on the wall above her bed. She's been wanting a big photo to go there for a long time.'

'You remember?' Kasturi looked surprised.

'Of course,' I nodded, and continued, 'And make a place for an indoor wooden swing.'

'Yes,' Kasturi slapped my shoulder, laughing. 'I was just going to mention that to her!'

Miraya and I exchanged a look, smiling in secret to one another.

'Kasturi,' Miraya said, 'I suppose I need to start afresh again. What else do you need?'

'Let me think …' Kasturi tapped a finger on her chin, looking to the sky with a thoughtful expression. 'I think I also mentioned having some sort of stand and pot-holder in a corner of my room at one point.'

'That's right!' Nodding I turned to Miraya to explain Kasturi's reason from long ago. 'She wanted a plant in the corner to bring the terrace to her room. It was her way of making up for not going there as often as I did.'

Miraya bit down on the end of her pencil a moment before nodding. 'I can work with that. In fact, I like that idea. A terrace-inspired room. Give me a moment to draw some of it up …'

'I should have invited you over to help us with this.' Kasturi hooked her arm in mine and heat hit my cheeks. 'Shaurya, I had no idea you knew me so well!'

The grin across my face made my cheeks ache. 'Kasturi, you're an amazing person. It would be a sin not to remember the things that make you happy.'

Miraya glanced up, flipping her page around. 'What about something like this?'

'Oh, I like it …' blinked Kasturi.

I hummed to myself a moment. 'But it needs more colours! Kasturi is always bright, her clothes are full of colours that dazzle your eyes.'

They laughed, everyone taking in the vivid blouse of yellow, orange and pink that she had on.

'Perhaps you know me too well …' Kasturi nudged herself into my shoulder. 'But I can't deny I would want more variety in colours.'

'No problem.' Miraya paused, taking in the way we were leaning into one another. 'You two are so cute …'

We both stiffened, breaking apart, and she laughed at the childish gesture. Looking at one another, Kasturi and I started laughing ourselves. I looked back at Miraya's sketches and ideas. One of the patterns stood out and I took it as a sign.

'Let's head to Mirza Ismail Road,' I motioned for them to follow me. 'I am pretty sure I saw some pottery with one of those patterns on them.'

'Really?' Miraya looked at the page as she gathered her materials up. 'I would be curious to see it now. Kasturi, can we go?'

'Absolutely!' she said. I was thrilled to have earned an outing with Kasturi.

It wasn't far to the markets that lined Mirza Ismail Road where I often rode to and from my classes. There were a lot more items than pottery sold there. Trinkets, food, and various handmade items filled the sides of the road where people traversed from one aspect of their life to the next. Over the sea of bouncing heads, I spotted a mountain-sized display of pottery. I gripped Kasturi's hand, and she in turn grabbed Miraya's, and I led us through the tides of travellers.

'Oh! I see it,' Miraya broke through at last, joining us inside the merchant's hovel. 'This is so close to what I was sketching ...'

She brought out her sketchbook, pulling a pencil from her hair to sketch the pattern next to her own. Kasturi and I leaned over her shoulders, watching the skilled and knowing flicks that left lines in such a perfect replica of what the pot held. It never seemed to bother Miraya if people watched her draw at such close quarters. Then again, I assumed with her line of work it was required to design and log a customer's wants and needs on the fly and in person.

'Do you like what you see?' It was the merchant who had come to see why we had crowded so intimately over the pot. 'Can I help you with anything?'

'Yes,' Miraya broke away, pushing herself in front of us. 'I really like this pattern, it's similar to my design and the look I was aiming for. Do you have anything else like that, or maybe close to what I have on this page here.'

His eyes dropped to her raised sketchbook and he rubbed his cheek. 'Hmm, you know … I might have something with those colours.'

'May I see it?' She looked over her shoulder at Kasturi and winked. 'I'm an interior designer from Mumbai. Perhaps we can work out a deal?'

'Come, come this way,' he smiled, leading them further into the inner reaches of his store, where rugs and pottery filled every crevice. 'I try to group them by colour in here. So please, take a closer look, make a list of what you like.'

'Thank you.' Miraya kneeled down in front of three jars, one larger than the other. 'Kasturi, look at these.'

'Oh!' She joined her, both the girls hovering over the blue-and-white patterned collection.

'You think Aunty would want these for her room?' She was checking for the maker's name and the price. 'They are a good price, and the company is well known.'

Kasturi looked them over before nodding in agreement. 'Even if she doesn't want all three in her room, it would be nice to use them to link the rooms together or even store stuff in the kitchen.'

'Oh, what a great idea …' Miraya signalled to the merchant. 'We'll take these for sure, but we're still looking.'

'I will pack those up while you shop, ma'am.' He took them up in his large arms and left them to continue to wander in and out of the shadows of his shop.

'What about this piece?' My eyes had found a colourful decorative pot with a vibrant mantra exploding from its base. 'These colours suit you, Kasturi. All the purple, orange, yellow, blue, and even silver lines breaking them up, like a kaleidoscope.'

'Shaurya, this is a wonderful piece.' Kasturi gripped my arm as she leaned in to take a closer look. 'Miraya, I really would love to incorporate all these colours in my room.'

Miraya rubbed her forehead and tapped her pencil against her sketchbook. 'But, my dear Kasturi, that's way more colours than you have walls. I'll have to find a clever way to do that … and not drown Aunty and Uncle with colours every time they step foot in your room.'

I laughed at the pout Kasturi gave her cousin. 'She didn't say no.'

A grin came back to her. 'You're right, that wasn't a no.'

Miraya nudged her shoulder. 'Come on, let's take these other jars back. Now I have some more ideas and we'll see if he can deliver some of these to me later when I am ready for them.'

21

MIRAYA'S DIARY

Shaurya doesn't just 'like' Kasturi; he's in love with her. The smile that graces his face when he reveals what he knows of her likes and dislikes is the brightest I have seen. This smile, unlike the ones I've seen before, isn't forced. Everything she has ever confided in him has never been forgotten, and watching that unfold today made even me smile.

I have forgotten this intimate and softer side of love. The excitement to hear someone speak the language of your soul in such a loving tone was something I enjoyed most. Like Shaurya said, 'It would be a sin not to remember the things that make you happy.'

He's right. When you find love, all that matters anymore is making the other person happy.

Seeing Kasturi and Shaurya, I question all the suspicions I have that are caused by my own past.

Is this love? Is it always this simple? I can't ... I don't know ... . I don't know if I can accept that as an answer or even as part of it just yet. My heart still bleeds. ...

22

SHAURYA

Miraya's voice startled me as I came down the stairs. 'Shaurya, can you please do me a favour?'

'Sure,' I said. 'What is it?'

'I need to get some materials for the work here. It's at a complete standstill until I do.' She looked over her shoulder towards Kasturi's house, flustered. 'No one else is home, not even Uncle or Aunty, and Kasturi is in college. You think you can take me to a shop nearby — if you're free, that is? Or at least give me some directions?'

'It's fine,' I said, descending the stairs, giving her a reassuring expression. 'I'm free at the moment and I have plenty of time before my classes start. Let's go.'

'Thank you so much! Hold on,' she said, motioning for me to wait. 'I need to grab my sketchbook!'

She dove back through the door and after a few minutes came out with a few papers, sketchbook and a pencil in hand. Locking the door, juggling her things, she joined me on the front pathway. I raised an eyebrow at the haphazard pile in her hands.

'I'm so sorry,' she breathed. 'I didn't want to keep you waiting so I just grabbed what I needed. Sorry ...'

'It's all right.' I chuckled. 'You can keep it in my bag.' I slid it off my shoulder and unzipped it for her.

'Thank you!'

'No problem.' She slid them in the bag and I closed it. 'It's fine. Keeping them in my bag frees up your hands and you won't lose them.'

'Definitely,' she nodded and rubbed her cheek. 'I need some hanging materials for pictures and wall décor. Besides that, I want to see if I can find things to fill some gaps in Aunty's room ... it still looks and feels so incomplete to me.'

I looked over at her from the corner of my eyes. 'How are things back home with you so far away?'

'They are all doing well.' She followed my lead as we made our way through the streets.

'You've been here in Jaipur for a while now. I barely know anything about you, Miraya.' I could see her face reddening, both of us remembering how she had pried my hidden information from me back on the terrace. A cunning smile crept across my lips. 'Tell me about yourself, your friends, even your *boyfriend*.'

'I don't have a boyfriend.' The twist in her lips told me the question irritated her.

There was a moment of silence. The atmosphere between us shifted, but my gut told me it wasn't from my question. I wondered if she had felt this drive for answers with me as I did now with her.

'I'm sorry.' It was the first thing I could think of to say, though it felt misplaced as it fell from my mouth.

'No, I was ...' she trailed off, as if nervous the next half would reveal her own secrets. 'I was actually thinking about the materials, sorry.'

'R-right.' I knew it was a lie. 'So, you went to college to be an interior decorator?'

'Yes.' A smile came back to her face. 'It was something I had always wanted to do. A lot of the family thought it was a bad idea, but I'm a rather stubborn creature at times. I chased after it and I can say it was well worth it.'

'Wow.' I marvelled over the idea of it. 'You're a brave person, Miraya. I couldn't imagine standing up against my family like that, and doing it alone.'

'I wasn't alone, the —' Again, a pause in her words and then a shift in conversation. 'Remind me I need materials to hang that huge picture in Kasturi's room ...'

Furrowing my brow, I saw that her eyes seemed to have glazed over. I knew that look well; I wore it on my face when visiting my own painful memories. She was avoiding saying something; but out of respect, I suppressed the urge to ask any further questions.

The shop was not much further, ending the awkward silence. Together we picked out some items I was sure Kasturi would like and we gathered the missing materials. It was amazing to see Miraya brighten, even glow, as she buzzed around the shop. She pulled the sketches from my bag, writing some things down on them while comparing the materials to her initial ideas. This is what she lived for, and to see her dive into her work was breathtaking. I wanted to be like that. To carry that shine in my eyes as I fulfilled a part of my dream, like Miraya did when sketching, planning, or even here, in the shop, picking out materials. Her soul emanated outward, warming the hearts near her. I wanted to feel that.

This, this is what it was like to be satisfied and doing what one loved. I yearned to feel that way when I finally got to do what I wanted — filmmaking! My heart swelled, a familiar ache slamming me as I watched her pay the cashier. Would that day ever come for me? My parents had gone as far as to find the idea silly and laughable. The stab of their reactions still made my heart and soul bleed. Not to mention the number of times my courage failed me, left me chained to the bench in the railway station. How awful to stop just when one was that close to leaving and chasing after one's dream.

Courage will follow, Kasturi's voice echoed through me. We were coming to her front stoop and I recovered from my thoughts. She had hope in me, despite the secrets I kept from her. Perhaps her encouragement was all I would ever need.

'Thank you so much, Shaurya,' Miraya said, taking her things out of my bag and pulling me from my thoughts. 'I will be able to get some work done while everyone is out thanks to you.'

'N-no problem.' Frowning, I failed to hold on to the few reassuring thoughts I had. 'I better get going … class will be starting soon.'

Nodding, we waved good-bye and, grabbing my bike, I set out on the path I knew so well. With each gear shift, I felt like I was drowning further into the depths of an empty future. The only people happy about this path were my parents, who understood nothing of the dreams one had. They had not been witness to the glow of a soul living its dream, like Miraya. How could they ever understand?

In bitter silence, I slid into my chair. Unzipping my bag, I froze. Blinking, I realized Miraya had left her diary back. I shuddered, a thought creeping forward with excitement. *I wonder what she writes in there with such passion.*

Shaking my head, I argued with myself. *She left it there by mistake. It must have slipped out between the sketches!*

True. It's a bad habit to read other people's diaries.

The other side of me chuckled, mocking my weakness against curiosity.

I'll return it to her tomorrow, I nodded to myself, digging myself further into the hole of mischief. *She surely only has some designs in there ...*

Sure! agreed the other side of my mind. *We don't even know if this is her personal journal. What harm would it be to read a page to confirm which she has left behind? If it is her personal diary, tomorrow is too long of a wait to return it to her, right?*

It was all I needed to break the last string keeping me from opening the diary. I flipped to a page, the ink and paper less worn than those before it. Huddling over it, I acted as if I were keeping my classmates from cheating off my test. My eyes widened as I read the words so elegantly scripted across the smooth paper.

~

For some reason I felt like writing today. It's been three months since I last sat down to write anything. But I experienced something interesting today. Something so surreal I cannot help but feel it needs to be written down.

Kasturi's neighbour and friend Shaurya is the same guy from the railway station. What are the odds? He was standing motionless ...

~

I pulled away after finishing the entry. Leaning back in my chair, I stared down at her writing, the beauty of it recalling a horrid moment in my own life. Miraya had said she saw me at the station, but I had no idea I'd stood by while her things had fallen around her. I rubbed the side of my jaw, a phantom slap for the taboos I had, and was presently performing, stinging. Did Kasturi know about this? Not only about my failure to help her at the railway station, but about the emotional pain and fear Miraya was struggling with?

My body tensed and I made up my mind. I flipped to the first page, wanting to know more about the life Miraya had run away from. She may be living her dream, but something was haunting her as much as my own failure to pursue my dreams was hurting me. I wanted to help her, much like she had started to help me recover my own resolve to pursue my dream of being a filmmaker. Maybe I could talk to Kasturi, find a way for both of us to pull ourselves from this tar pit of despair.

Oh my God. I couldn't believe I'd stood there and let all of Miraya's wonderful sketches blow away with the wind. How blind was I? If I had known — no — I should have snapped out of it, scrambled to help her like a decent person. Instead I had walked away, how horrible! No wonder she was aggressive and abrasive! *But I will make it right, Miraya,* I thought to myself. *If only you had said something to me sooner. No, you tried, but I was too ashamed to admit I had failed to chase after my dream to see what it was you were trying to say. I'm so sorry, Miraya.*

23

MIRAYA'S DIARY

Mumbai

I can't believe it! Mohit finally proposed! We've been together since college, and I was starting to wonder if this day would ever happen. And finally, when it happened, it was like a dream!

He took me out on a date, and the chemistry was surreal before I even realized why we were there. The restaurant was amazing; I think the name of it was Terttulia? It was cute, intimate and the food mind-blowing! I loved the angles inside and the use of different furniture to make each section stand out. We left the restaurant holding hands, enjoying the shops we passed until we found ourselves in front of one of the arches at Chaitya Bhoomi.

The ocean breeze felt wonderful and the lights on the Sea Link were surprisingly romantic. He said my name, so soft, and when I turned from the railing, he was on one knee. My heart felt as if it was going to pop out of my chest! He held up a small box that was open to reveal a ring so beautiful it brought tears to my eyes.

Before he could even finish asking, I was screaming yes! I fell down into his arms, kissing him over and over.

~

We had dinner with my parents to celebrate landing my first independent project as an interior designer. They are proud of me for once. So many times I have faced their frowning faces when I brought up this dream, but now, they aren't afraid to smile about it. I suppose they didn't want to see me get hurt if I failed while pursuing this dream. After all, I am their baby girl. Who can blame them?

But yes! Have I told you about my first official job as an interior designer? To be honest, Mohit did pull some strings to get me the job. He told me to consider it as a wedding gift. I have never been so happy! My dream is coming to life before me, my parents are proud of me for it, and I am marrying the love of my life. Mohit has helped me every step of the way, and I cannot be happier that I will soon become his wife!

My parents are thrilled that he finally proposed. Tomorrow I meet the client and start living my dream!

~

Tomorrow I will officially be Mohit's wife. My college sweetheart, the love of my life, my everything. I get to look forward to waking up to his smile every morning and hear the honeyed words fall from his loving lips day in and day out. My heart races at the thought!

My wedding gown is magnificent! The design is a mixture

of traditional Indian styling with the classic bride-in-white flair along with a matching headdress. I will look like a goddess when Mohit sees me in it. His smile will be one I cannot shake from my memory. My heart and soul will speak those vows, knowing we both have lived by them before this point and will always be true to one another for the rest of our lives.

The idea of sharing his last name gives me a sense of completion, much like when my first client requested for me to come back for another job. This was my other dream. So many girls aren't as lucky as I am — to be able to marry their college sweetheart. OH! I must go and get ready for the dance rehearsal!

~

I feel lost. Confused, even. Mohit, he doesn't smile anymore. Not at me, anyhow. Each time our eyes meet, he frowns and looks away. I don't understand it. I can't help but feel there's a huge amount of resentment in the way he's acting. Did I, have I done something to make him feel that way?

He stays out late after work … it could be he's overworking himself? I don't know. I've been so busy with all the jobs I am handling, it feels like I am coming home to a stranger who looks like Mohit. He sighs a lot; his shoulders are heavy with the way he carries himself. I ask, 'What's wrong, Mohit?', and I get a sharp, 'Nothing', before he leaves the room.

My gut churns with each wave of strange behaviour. As his wife, I should be able to help him through this, through whatever is eating him up inside. But then that fearful thought keeps me tossing and turning at night that it might be me. I've made him *unhappy, lost the ability to make him smile. He no longer tries to make me smile in the ways he did barely a year ago ... this hurts and I can't seem to stop it.*

~

Mohit is jealous. At first, I didn't see it. Those resentful looks were a mild precursor to the degrading and bitter words he spits at me now. I thought I had upset him somehow, but then it continued no matter how hard I tried to make him happy. Each time, he lashes out in the direction of my career. The dream that he helped create is now a curse to him ... and I am to blame.

It's wrong. Where is the encouraging man I married? The college sweetheart who gifted me my very first foot in the door to reach my dream career? How happy we were at that time, he was so proud of me. Here I sit, years later, when I thought life would be enriching and rewarding. Instead, I am met with a forked-tongued doppelganger when I come home and worse when I wake every morning.

I can't remember the last time I saw him smile. The only time I smile is while I am working, but his double-edged words are starting to reach me even there. I can't give up on being an interior designer. I love my job, and my reputation is now known all over Mumbai. And I don't understand Mohit's jealousy. We are husband and wife, everything we do is to make the other person proud. Why is he breaking me down after helping me reach this dream?

I think I will ask him. We need to talk; we need to stop this merry-go-round of malicious words and constant abandonment.

Today I found myself waiting here at the kitchen table. He was supposed to be home for dinner. I made his favourite, but it's cold now. Worse, he's not picking up his phone ... where did my beloved Mohit go?

~

Fights. No more calm discussions, no more gentle talks. We fight every time one of us opens our mouth to the other. I feel like I've been caught in an explosion, shell-shocked.

Today he asked me to quit my job. I was floored, insulted. When I pressed further, he demanded I settle down and have a child. It stung. Never have we discussed this before, even after marrying. I feel like this deep desire of his grew in his silence and is now bursting from him in a monstrous rage.

It made me angry. How dare he demand I quit my job! Is this his way of taking me completely out of my dream career? This isn't what I wanted! I, I feel like he lifted me up like a trophy and now that I've outgrown my shelf he wants to throw me away. Replace me with something neither of us wanted in all the years we've been together. I don't understand! The words and the way he demands that I give up all that makes me who I am — my career, my future, everything. It's insulting and disrespectful. I am his wife! Yet, somehow, I feel that he thinks I've outgrown him; that he wants me to fall silent now. It's cruel ...

But, part of me is scared. Am I really going to keep my marriage in such a bitter place for the sake of self-respect? How can I justify which evil is the lesser one: sacrificing my life or my marriage? Why is Mohit making me choose? Where did the love that he once held for me go? I haven't seen that man, my beloved, in those eyes for far too long. ...

I can only pray that the fighting dissipates. If we talk this out, reveal our desires, I am sure we can find some middle ground. There are plenty of women in Mumbai who work and have children. Why is this not an option? Why does he twist his face with such rage when I even suggest this?

~

I'm getting a divorce. An ugly word, it leaves an ugly sensation on my soul and heart. This was not what I wanted. But Mohit, he ...

Mohit slapped me. My cheek bruised, my very being still stings with the heaviness of it. It felt like a brick slamming into my left cheek. The pain shocking, I folded over, gripping the throbbing in my face, gasping in pain. Wide-eyed, tears fell across the sidewalk where we were.

He was walking out the door. I chased after him, insisting I wanted to go with him to his friend's dinner party. He's been going to them a lot, yet never naming who it is, and at times not coming home until morning. I, I couldn't watch him leave me alone in that cold, loveless house again.

I grabbed his sleeve, pleading, 'Mohit, I'm going with you. I'm your wife!'

His palm smashed into my face, and as I was bent over in shock, I heard his bitter hiss, 'As my wife, you need to learn your place ...'

I heard his steps leave me there, broken and vulnerable. My heart aching, I knew I could not dare to stay another day in what used to be my home. Locking that door felt like I was locking my own cage. I can't tell you how long I sobbed with my forehead against my own door. The moment I stepped away, I knew my marriage would be over.

By the time I made it to my parents, my cheek had swollen, the colour a horrendous maroon turning purple. Never did I want to feel my husband's strength in this manner. The hands that had been so tender and gentle with me ... held out a ring to me with promises that he had now broken without guilt ...

My parents have given me their approval. I will be divorcing Mohit. My marriage, my wonderful love, are nothing more than shattered pieces on the ground at my feet.

~

I've had it with love ... it's a false and dreadful thing. It makes you feel safe, and when you need it the most, it abandons you. I will not let it betray me again, ever again. In fact, I've had it with being close to people. Divorcing Mohit has ripped away even people I thought were my friends. From here on, I will focus on my career. It's the only thing that hasn't bitten my hand.

And writing, what good have you done me? I wrote to you, desperate for your help, your counsel, and you did nothing. This is the last time I give you the pleasure to sit there idly and watch my life fall apart. This story of my life ends here. No more love stories, no more tales of my achievements. I am content to live for myself and end this story written in this useless book.

24

SHAURYA

Jaipur

I sat there, shocked. Miraya had been through so much. Her life had unfolded like a rose. But when she gripped it tight, the thorns had torn into her soul and left her bleeding as all the petals fell to the ground. Tears welled in the corners of my eyes. I needed to talk to her and make up for being another sour point in her life when she was hurting so much from her life in Mumbai.

The lecture passed by like a leaf floating in a stream. None of the professor's words reached my mind while I was looking so far ahead, waiting for time to inch forward so I could confront Miraya.

By the time I made it to the terrace of our building, I was breathless. I tried to calm myself, though I feared Miraya wouldn't show, and the minutes felt like they were hours ticking by. My heart swelled as she finally came into the private space.

Rising to my fight, I took my chance to change both our lives. 'Miraya, you need to change your life. Give it a second chance. The story of your life shouldn't end on such a bitter note.'

'Wh-what?' She looked at me, lost in the words.

'You left this in my bag.' I handed the diary to her, holding my breath for the outrage I knew would come.

'You … you read my diary!' Jerking it from my hand, her jaw tightened with the rise of her anger. 'How dare you! You have no right to do something like that! You, you …'

'Miraya, I know … you have every right to be angry with me.' My face was stern and it made her flinch. 'Listen, I know everything now, I understand what's been going on …'

'How could you …' Tears were starting to fall from her eyes.

'You have to change your story. Don't end it there with everything falling apart around you.' I was fighting back my own tears. 'You're my friend, and to think such horrible things have come to pass in your life is heartbreaking. It was unexpected but you did what you could to fix it. You need to continue, change the ending … this, there in that book, *this is not your story.*'

'You have no right to tell me this!' She hugged her diary tight, shaking her head in denial. 'Someone like you, who can't follow his dream, can't confess his love to Kasturi! You have no right to want to change my life; *this is not your story*, Shaurya.'

'I … I am a coward, unlike you, Miraya.' My shoulders slumped. 'You have the power to change your life, but I have failed … you've seen that look on my face, watching the train.'

'If you are brave enough to get to the station, why don't you let yourself follow through?' she hissed. 'Instead you stood there like a fool even while I was struggling … and here you stand telling me what to do? You can't even tell Kasturi how you feel about her!'

'That has nothing to do with this …' I balled up my fist. 'And had I known it was you at the station, it, it would have been different.'

'Really?' Her brow furrowed with her disbelief. 'So some other girl would have found herself in the same situation — a man slamming into her while another just watches her work fly away forever.'

'I was lost. I was afraid …' I closed my eyes, the sensation of the chains from the bench coming back across my soul. 'You don't know what it is to have parents who don't believe in you, that want you to be content with the same life they live. To feel the chains of your self-doubt tighten in that one moment when you should have been able to make your dreams come true!'

'I do, Shaurya,' she spat without missing a beat. 'And

what is it that stops you from confessing to Kasturi that you *love* her? You can't blame your parents for that.'

I didn't know how to answer that. Fuelled by rage and despair, I stomped past her, leaving her on the terrace. As I crossed the threshold of my front door, I could hear Miraya's angry footsteps on the terrace. The door clicked to a close and I leaned back on it. I covered my face in shame: I had managed to push a friend away and make matters worse for her and me. All I'd wanted to do was help, but Miraya had a point. How could I help when I was unwilling to fix my own problems?

For me, it had seemed easy and clear what she should do — not give up. But I was the one who needed to take that advice; I needed to not give up on my life and settle for this dissatisfying ending I'd given myself. The night my parents shot my dreams down, I was feeling rebellious, but the empty frame on my wall was an acceptance of my giving up. No, that was not what I had intended. The frame was the person I hadn't become yet, the person I wanted to be would fill that frame someday, but staying in Jaipur guaranteed it stayed empty. That was the truth.

I felt terrible for Miraya, but she was right. How could I push her to change her story when I refused to take the steps needed to change my own? Falling on the bed, my thoughts circled round and round again, from Miraya's words to her diary. In some place between them were the answers as to what to do about my own problems.

25

MIRAYA'S DIARY

Is this really not my story?

Shaurya thinks he is a coward, but only a brave man could have done what he did today on the terrace. What else could drive someone to confess they read a diary and then go as far as pushing the person who wrote it to change their lives?

To be honest with myself, it has felt good to start again in Jaipur. Here there are no reminders of him. People are encouraging and friendly, no one here has endured the rumours or seen the fall of my marriage. Shaurya may have overstepped, but it doesn't mean his words were wrong.

Give my life a second chance …

I can start again in Jaipur. This time I am making my own career, standing on my own two feet, unlike my life before. A new beginning to a new story, not a chapter tacked on to the end of the last one.

Shaurya, though — he's a mess; so eager to help a friend, yet unable to fix his own dilemmas. I want to help him break those chains of self-doubt, but like him, I will have to break my own first. It felt wrong to be arguing in the terrace like that, but I was riding a wave of anger. My precious diary, you betrayed me yet again.

Then again, you are only a book that holds the story I place inside your pages. ...

26

ANUBHAV

Bangalore

For weeks, I wandered the streets. I had been sleeping in my office since I had failed to pay rent at my flat. I had the money, but no desire to make the effort to withdraw it from the bank.

It was hard to tell me apart from a homeless man, but then again, I had become one. I had allowed myself to fall to such a lowly place in society with no sense of shame. Before, I drank to drown the grief, but at this stage, I was drinking to stay drunk. Being sober made it too obvious what I had done to myself, to my dream, to my life.

My neat haircut grew ragged, my clean-shaven face was marred by an uneven, greying beard, filled with random bits from food I managed to force in.

Ruined and broken, I begged for coins and counted

them obsessively until I got that magic number to grab another bottle from the store.

'My God, what happened to you?' The voice was as if from a dream, but looking up I realized it was someone standing in front of me. 'What on earth could make someone fall this low?'

I know that voice. My thoughts scrambled desperately through the kaleidoscope of memories to place where I knew him from.

He was someone important. A symbol of my success, somehow. But who? Not a co-worker, surely; I would have recognized him even in my state. A former classmate then? Someone from another company that my venture had dealt with?

Somehow, my inebriated mind managed to reach out and grasp his identity. The man outside the building ... the man I swore I would have lunch with when I was successful and we worked in the same skyscraper.

I was mortified. One minute, I was bragging about my ambitions; the next, I was begging the very same man for loose change to help me live.

I wasn't sure if he was asking me or himself, but an alcohol-laden voice from my chapped lips obliged. 'Parents dead, my own company abandoned me, and now I drink away the last of my sorry life.'

He grimaced as my laughter changed to coughing. 'Go home. Find yourself again.'

I froze, a moment of sobriety shook through me. 'Find … myself?'

'You had dreams.' He shoved money in my palm and we locked eyes. 'Go home and find them again.'

'No!' I heard my own voice shout. 'My dreams are gone. This … story of my life … it is gone.'

The man shook his head. 'You're letting life write your story. But you can control how that story is written; rather than allow it to be created for you.'

I took one of the hundred-rupee notes he had given me and held it up. 'I am the other side of this note now. You see the same me you met outside this building. I look the same, but I am changed.'

He smiled sadly. 'No matter how you flip that money around,' he said, nodding to the note in my hand, 'it is still worth something. You can crumple it up, rip it in half. But once it's smoothed out or taped up again, it is the same. It can still buy sustenance.'

'I don't know,' I muttered. The anger had left me once again and I was just a broken man. Exhausted with life.

The stranger continued. 'It will be hard, but at some point you will understand that your story is your own. Then you can move forward and keep creating it. You are a strong man, my friend. I don't know what happened to you, but you have the strength to change your circumstances.'

He closed my hand around the money. 'This should be enough to get you home.'

Looking down at the money, tears dropped from my eyes and fell against it. I looked up to thank the stranger, but he was gone, vanished, as if some sort of guardian angel. What stopped me from using the money for alcohol, I'm not sure, but I did buy a train ticket to Jaipur.

So, with my tail between my legs, I went home. Hands shaking, it took a long time before I could bear to unlock the front door of my childhood home. Relics of my parents were all still in place, as if they would be coming home any minute.

Time felt stagnant, sitting there at the kitchen table or even in the living room. I found myself looking at the door, waiting, hoping it was all a bad dream, and that I would see them walk in. Smiles on their faces, they'd fuss over the idea that I'd got too drunk and had to crash on their couch. Dad would ask how the business was doing and I wouldn't have to see his smile fade because I'd given it all up over a bottle of booze.

27

SHAURYA

Jaipur

It had been a week since Miraya and I argued on the terrace. We hadn't spoken a single word to each other since then. I would see her on the stoop, but I lacked the courage to talk to her. Which added to my anxiety when Kasturi called to ask me to come with them to Amer Fort. I had said yes without hesitation, forgetting the situation. But as soon as I hung up, I wondered how it would be between Miraya and me.

The Amer Fort was very popular with tourists as well as a wedding venue. On a hill, the orange hue of the walls of the great fortress stretched wide. Tall facades lined the right side of the building, while a grand archway formed the entrance in the centre of its greatness. Despite our last encounter, Miraya and I did not let any tension show in front of Kasturi. And soon we all found ourselves marvelling over the beauty of the palace within the walls.

Miraya couldn't stop smiling. With her pencil and sketchbook, she took any chance she could to sketch out the magnificent sights. Kasturi led the way out of the courtyard filled with geometrical shapes and paths laid in such a way it sucked you into the centre. The palace held more intricate and beautiful patterns. Images of gods and goddesses were still vivid, while the repeating and mesmerizing mosaics of plants and flowers seemed to never end.

A few times, taken in by the beauty of the place, Kasturi would cling to my arm, and my heart fluttered. Miraya would eye me as I turned to Kasturi, my mouth agape, but courage gone. She was right. Until I told Kasturi that I liked her, I would have to be content with being a close friend.

We wandered from one room filled with dark blue, orange, green and red to another of teal, pink, and orange. Each depicting flowers, each devoted to its own theme. Through the structure within, while the decorative lines laid out across the walls and up the dome ceiling were identical in symmetry, it was breathtaking to see how different from one another they remained.

Time was flying, and our stomachs were growing empty. Kasturi brought up the topic of food, and Miraya and I found ourselves laughing over her one-track mind. We were reluctant to leave such a wonderful place though.

I had been there so many times, but seeing Miraya's face light up and be inspired by it changed it for me.

The cliffs grew dark as the sunlight faded. We were starting our descent when Kasturi paused. Blinking, I turned to where she was looking. The wind howled as my eyes fell on a man standing some distance from us, his toes off the edge of the plateau, his face taut, his eyes glazed. A shiver went down my spine.

28

ANUBHAV

Jaipur

Despite the stranger's optimism, I knew I was nothing but a piece of trash, throwing everything I had left to the gutters.

With the memories of my loving parents everywhere I turned, my drinking increased once I was home. Moving to a hotel didn't help. Broken beyond anything I ever imagined, I found myself at the very place I proclaimed I would be king. Amer Fort, where my parents dreamed I would one day get married. …

But what woman would want a drunken fool such as me? Even the beauty of Amer Fort could not hide that. …

Echoes from the past crept in and out as I staggered through the beautiful place. Finally I ran down to where I could peer beyond the railing to the cliff's edge. The wind whistled, hissing my dark failures and thoughts to me. I climbed under the railing and I shared my last bottle with it. I laughed a little over the fall of the bottle. It smashed far below as my toes dangled over the lip of eternal death.

It was here that it whispered, *Jump, Anubhav.*

I wonder ... I muttered back, smiling.

You can make all this pain go away! it promised in the next updraft that rocked me, threatening to pull me over. *Find your parents again on the other side!*

My parents ... I sighed, staring with a forlorn look in my eyes down to where the bottle had smashed. *I miss them* ...

You're nothing but trash! Come! Join the rest of the trash here in the ravine! Whistling, another draft rocked me on my heels and I laughed.

Patience, wind! I lit a cigarette and stared out over the horizon with a cold emptiness. *I will come after I smoke my last cigarette.*

When I was done, I threw it down the ravine, and the gentle tug and whisper promised me, *Just open your arms and welcome death!*

29

SHAURYA

'Is he taking a selfie?' Kasturi's voice was a mere whisper, filled with uncertainty. 'A stunt junkie?'

'No ...' I shook my head, my eyes unable to break from the man. 'Look at him, look at his face. He's alone and deep in thought. ...'

'Is, is he ...' Kasturi tugged the back of my shirt, sending chills across my skin. 'Is he going to jump? Is he going to commit suicide?'

'We need to stop him.' Miraya hugged her sketchbook.

My mind raced and I motioned for the two of them to stay back, knowing the man may not be thinking or acting rationally. I was nervous that shouting out to the man might startle him, send him into a panic, and cause him to jump out of desperation that his task would be prevented. Approaching the edge, I swallowed back my nerves. My head spun looking down at the depths and I refocused on the man. Taking my steps slowly, one at a time, I inched toward him. He was finishing the last of his cigarette; a sway in his body made my stomach lurch. A stream of smoke rolled from his lips as he flicked the cigarette butt into the wind. His eyes were closing, his arms raising outward; he was ready to jump!

As if lightning had struck every muscle inside me, I leapt forward, gripped the man's arm, and pulled him away from the edge. As I dragged him back under the railings, he hollered and cursed at me. The man was drunk, and his words were slurred. Kasturi and Miraya had rushed over, ready to help in any way they could. I was panting where I sat, pale-faced, watching him wrestle with invisible demons.

'Wh-what the hell were you doing?' I exclaimed, my pulse roaring in my ears.

'Get lost!' another drunken bellow started. 'Who are you! Who are you to stop me!'

'Sir!' pleaded Kasturi. 'We just saved your life! Do you … do you need help? We can help you.'

'Listen you …' He sat up, swaying in his drunkenness and peering at us through bloodshot eyes. 'You don't even know me. Don't pretend to be a friend … I couldn't care less who you are … LEAVE-ME-ALONE …'

We watched as he tried a few times to get back on his feet. It had been a miracle he hadn't fallen before we came along. I rose to my feet, ready to fight him if he tried again, and he tried to shove me to the side. All he accomplished was that he stumbled backward and fell back to the ground. Relief washed over me and I folded, leaning on my knees, trying to catch my breath and slow my heart. Miraya handed her sketchbook to Kasturi and, with inspiring calm, she knelt next to the man and took his hand.

'We are not going anywhere.' Her voice was solid, the tone emerging from her lips like words from the man's own mom.

'No! Just …' He was still angry, but his voice whimpered with each outcry. 'Just leave me alone!'

'You mean, to let you jump.' I looked at him, baffled. 'Leave you alone to die.'

'Yes, that's it. I want to die.' Tears were pouring down his rage-filled face. 'I am nobody. Especially to you. Why are you interfering with my life! LEAVE ME ALONE!'

Miraya shook her head. 'We might be nobody to you, and you nobody to us, but you are definitely somebody to someone. Just because you are no longer interested in your life, it doesn't mean someone in it will let you throw it away so easily. That is why we are interfering with your life.'

'I couldn't stand the thought of letting someone die in front of me,' Kasturi started to cry, hugging Miraya's sketchbook for comfort. 'Not like that …'

The man rummaged through his pockets; pulling out

a cigarette and lighter, he lit another one and took a long draw from it. 'Then it's simple. Walk away. I never asked you to watch.'

'Shut up!' The shout startled us all. It was Kasturi. 'We are going nowhere without you!'

'Why don't you understand …' Again the drunken whine and tears flooded out of him, his cigarette bouncing between his lips as he spoke. 'I don't have anything or anyone to live for! I am nothing … I never wanted anything from life.'

I came over to sit on the other side of the man and handed him what was left of the bottle of water I was carrying. 'Here, drink this. It'll help clear your head. Tell us who you are and what happened with you.'

After a long moment of silence, he finished the cigarette and the water. Sighing, he took in our faces with a scowl across his face. Sighing again so heavily you would think a great amount of boulders were stacked on his shoulders, he started to tell us his story.

'I don't know who you are, but I'm Anubhav, and this is my story …'

30

SHAURYA

Anubhav's tears fell heavy as he completed his story, dripping from his chin, staining his shirt. Shaken, he lit yet another cigarette. Sucking it into life, he gave us all a deeper, more sober glare. Exhaling, he blew the rolling smoke from his lips and he locked eyes with me, as if seeing his reflection within them.

'Now you see what I've been struggling with …' He took another puff of his cigarette before he finished, '… and why I just … just leave me alone.'

Narrowing my eyes, I declared, 'You've given us more reasons to stay with you, Anubhav.'

'Shaurya's right, we can't walk away knowing you're in so much pain.' Kasturi wiped a tear from her cheek. 'I'm so sorry about your parents. …'

There was a long silence as he smoked his cigarette. He had calmed down; even his voice had become softer.

His words felt less abrasive; they were no longer being shouted in a drunken slur. I couldn't help but wonder if being able to pour his soul out in words to a couple of strangers had caused this shift. How long had he gone around carrying this monstrous amount of sorrow and broken dreams inside him? In just a short amount of time — perhaps an hour or two had passed — he had recovered a little. Anubhav's demeanour, physically and spiritually, had changed to a less desperate one. Still, none of us would be leaving the cliff side without him.

'Anubhav, I know what happened to you …' Miraya's voice caught everyone's attention and she searched for the right words to convey what she wanted to the broken man before us. 'It wasn't fair. You have every right to feel negative and downcast after all that came crashing down on you. But is death really the solution?'

'I can't stop the pain …' Covering his face, his voice trembled as he confessed. 'At least if I were dead, it would stop. I wouldn't hurt any more. …'

'No! You're wrong! You'll cause the same pain to people in your life; you'll pass it on.' Anger boiled up in me, my voice strong. 'Anubhav, you must give your life a second chance! Don't let your story end like this! *This is not your story*, the one where you fall to your death can never be a story anyone wants to be a part of!'

Miraya nodded. 'If you keep lamenting over your past, you can never build your future!'

'I don't want a future,' Anubhav retorted.

'That's not true,' I insisted. 'Everyone wants to live. That is the natural way.'

Kasturi spoke up. 'You can be afraid, depressed. Life can be unfair. I think the easier thing is to give up — it is far harder to keep going. Find the strength.'

Miraya grabbed Anubhav by the shoulders and gave him a little shake. 'She's right. It is easy to die. It takes more strength than you even realize to keep living. But dig down into your soul and pull that courage up from the depths. It's there. You need to find it.'

I watched the two women volley their comments back and forth without giving Anubhav a breath to argue. Despite the seriousness of the situation, I desperately wanted to laugh as Miraya and Kasturi shot comment after comment at him.

'Life can knock you down like a stone falling from the sky with no warning,' Miraya continued. 'You have to hold on to the belief that it will get better.'

'Yes,' Kasturi insisted. 'There is a great storm in your heart right now, but the rain will stop and the clouds will clear. You will see the sun again.'

Anubhav grunted. 'That's easy for you to say. You aren't me, you haven't lived my life.'

'How do you know that I have not walked the same path of pain?' Miraya looked to me, following my lead, her words heartfelt. 'I can only say this with such confidence because I have, Anubhav. Shaurya is right. Life always deserves a second chance, a chance to make things better. I didn't think so, not until he confronted me and made me realize this.'

Anubhav's hands fell away from his face and he looked at Miraya. His eyes searched hers as if looking for those familiar signs of torment. I felt proud to hear her words, to know the rush of courage I'd had to confront her had made a change in how she looked at her own life. Now, it was her turn to change someone else's life around, remind them to choose life over death. For once, I was making a difference in the world around me. Anubhav's brow furrowed in recognition and Miraya continued her plea.

'You wanted to die, right? Jump over the cliff and wash away your life?' He nodded, confused by her words at first. 'Consider this: your old life did jump and has died here and now. This moment, these laboured breaths you take now are the start of a new life, like you were born again right where you sit. Like taking the first steps, start everything all over again, Anubhav.'

Again, Kasturi echoed Miraya's words. 'Some stories are hidden deep within you. You just need to find them.'

Miraya squeezed his shoulder gently. 'It takes tremendous bravery to even decide to live. But I see that strength in you. Write yourself a new story, okay?'

The tears fell slower, and the affectionate advice Miraya had bestowed on him seemed to engulf his soul in warmth he had forgotten existed in the world. Watching him, I reflected that light to the life I myself had lived to this point. If I could make Miraya change her life and this man's, why wasn't I changing my own? She was able to take my words to heart, but I still needed to heed my own advice. Anubhav's eyes fell to the ground, his frown deepened on his face.

With a great heave, his voice low, he said, 'But I have no idea what I should do now.'

'Come with us,' I smiled, patting his shoulder to bring his gaze back to me. 'Come join us for dinner, and maybe we can help you figure that out too.'

Another wave of tears was forming in his eyes as he took my hand in his and I pulled him back to his feet. 'O-okay. I will ...'

By the time we made it down the pathway, we had managed to earn a smile and laugh out of Anubhav. It was proof we were getting his mind to move in a better direction than it had been when he loomed over the cliff side. The fluorescent lights of a nearby restaurant gave Anubhav a daunting appearance. He was very thin, and stress lines ran deep in his face and around his sunken eyes. I couldn't help but wonder when he had last eaten or even slept. My heart ached to see someone in such a state, even after achieving his dreams. Could this happen to me? Could this have been my story?

'Anubhav, where are you staying?' Kasturi asked, her words cautious in tone. 'Do you need a place to stay?'

He shook his head. 'No, I'm staying in a hotel at the moment. I, I couldn't bear being at my parents' house.'

'I understand.' I motioned to the waiter to bring our bill. 'If you want, you can crash at my place.'

Swallowing the food in his mouth, he shook his head again. 'You've done too much already. Saved my life and even fed me. I couldn't bear being any more of a bother.'

'But we're still scared for you.' Miraya's stern face hit both of us. 'Shaurya, would you mind accompanying Anubhav? Make sure he makes it to the hotel safe?'

I looked to Anubhav, who gave no signs of refusal. 'I can do that.'

'Thank you, Shaurya.' Kasturi smiled and my heart raced. 'You're such a kind soul.'

I grinned, 'Not as kind as you, Kasturi.'

After paying for the dinner, I waved goodbye to the girls. Kasturi was smiling, her lips silently mouthing a *thank you* before she turned away. The walk to the nearby hotel was quiet. Both of us were nervous, but I followed him without hesitation. We may have saved him from the cliff but, like Miraya and Kasturi, I too feared he might try something again. He seemed happier after getting to know us better, having had a chance to smile and laugh in good company. He unlocked the hotel room door, holding it open for me.

The room was dark and gloomy. Beer cans and liquor bottles were scattered all over the tiny square box. A smell emanated throughout the room, a mixture of an overfilled ashtray, alcohol, and body odour. Closing the door, Anubhav turned and rubbed the side of his jaw, as if looking at the mess without clouded eyes for the first time. Grabbing the tiny garbage can, he stumbled from one piece of trash to the next, chucking it into the bucket. Feeling great sorrow for him, I joined in the process until we couldn't fit anything else into the trashcan.

'I'm sorry,' he mumbled, too ashamed to look me in the eyes. 'I've really let myself go.'

'It's okay,' I said gently. 'After what you told me, I can't say I wouldn't find myself doing the same.'

He gave me a half-hearted smile. 'Thank you.'

Nodding, I sat in the only chair in the room. 'Anyway, you don't have to apologize to me. All I ask is you give life a second chance, Anubhav.'

Rubbing the back of his neck, he looked towards the bathroom. 'I'm going to go clean up. I smell like a homeless man. You can leave if you want …'

'I'll be out here.' I gave him a grave expression, making it clear I would not leave him by himself to attempt anything again. 'You're not alone in the world, remember that.'

Sighing, he nodded his acknowledgment of the fact. When the bathroom door opened again, steam rolling out, he looked more alive than he had all night. Shuffling to his bed, he landed belly down onto the mattress, gripping his pillow in his arms. He began snoring a minute later, though the muscles in his back remained tense. He had a long fight ahead of him. It wouldn't be any easier for him to start life over again than it was for me to board the train to Mumbai.

Smirking, I muttered under my breath, 'At least the alcohol did you one favour. I don't think you would have slept so soundly otherwise. ...'

31

MIRAYA'S DIARY

Today was one of the most terrifying moments of my life. When we were at the fort, we encountered a man on a cliff on the verge of committing suicide. It must have been fate for us to be walking by when we did. No one else was around, no one else seemed to pass before or after the whole ordeal.

You can't imagine how sick I felt to realize how close we were to not seeing him. If we had spent more time looking at another part of the fort, he would be dead now.

How can someone be that finished with life?

My heart is still racing.

Shaurya managed to pull him away just before he let himself fall. His name is Anubhav, and to say he is a man in great internal pain would be putting it mildly.

My heart broke as he began to speak.

The story of his life fell from his lips as if he were desperate to get rid of its weight. This man has been through a lot; after making his dream job a reality, he lost both his parents. As he lost himself to sorrow and alcohol, he was cut out of his own business and he spiralled out of control.

The poor man. His family died and his own company turned their back on him. He had nobody to care whether he lived or died!

I had to do something, say something in the hope of making a difference in his life. Shaurya's words were still fresh in my mind. The idea to start again, to give life a second chance. I saw a little of myself in Anubhav. It terrified me, and the thought that I almost watched someone die sends chills through me. I pleaded for him to start again, to write a new story for his life. In his eyes, I shared the same pain he had.

There are no words for achieving your dream, your career of a lifetime, and then have those you looked forward to sharing that experience with get ripped away. Looking back, I wonder if it would have been easier if … if Mohit had just died and left me widowed and not divorced. Seeing Anubhav, I know it would have been soul-crushing. I would have found myself next to him ready to leap off that cliff, rather than losing myself in my work.

Anubhav couldn't look to his job as a means to keeping his head above the drowning waters of depression. And when they cut him from the company, the last inkling of hope was stripped from him. It scares me that I could have been like Anubhav.

Looking back, I am ashamed at how bitter I was at first to have Shaurya be so bold as to confront me, insulted that he had read my diary. Now, after some time has passed, I have soaked in his words and the message he was driven to beat into me there on the terrace. I realize that you, Diary, hold the relics of my old story and I was the author, the pen writing it, and therefore I've always had the power to change it.

Part of me feels childish to think I leaned on a book, on these pages, to call out answers or change what was happening. Regardless, today I passed on that drive to live again!

Like Shaurya did for me, I demanded Anubhav give life a second chance! To let himself be born again, start with his first steps all over again and not let his story end with such a horrific dive off that cliff.

Yes, we saved his life. But it is now up to him to begin living it again. There is a lesson in today's events for everyone. Especially me.

32

SHAURYA

We were venturing into April, summer time, and its daunting heat built up in the early afternoon hours, bringing distorting waves off cars. Still, it did not seem to affect Anubhav, who was smiling more and more every day. The man I had met two weeks ago was no longer present in the one sitting across the café table from me. He looked healthy: no more dark circles under his eyes; and the colour had returned to his face. Granted, he had trouble keeping to this new path, and had stumbled off it a few times.

My eyes fell to Anubhav's left forearm, which had bandages wrapped around it. A few days after taking him back to his hotel, he was still drinking. Not as much, but enough for him to be filled with self-loathing — I had caught him burning himself with his cigarettes. It was a grisly smell and sight. I could feel the burns on my own arm at the thought of it. When I told Miraya and Kasturi about it, Miraya demanded I take her to his hotel room.

I stood in awe at the way she was able to pull Anubhav back from the edge once more, just like she had done at Amer Fort. Her words reached his soul the loudest, and at times, I could hear my own flow from her.

I smiled to hear her say softly, 'We choose to change our life path; it does not happen by chance.'

Sitting here at the café, you would think the two of them were a couple. Anubhav smiled the widest when it was Miraya talking to him. This was probably the same smile I had on my face when talking to Kasturi. He clung to her; she had become part of the reason he was giving life a second chance.

'How long are you planning to stay in the hotel, Anubhav?' I asked.

He rubbed the back of his neck, thinking. 'I'm not sure. I suppose I should work on prepping my parents' place so it can be sold. Move in some place smaller, or buy a decent condo of sorts.'

'Miraya is an excellent interior designer,' Kasturi patted Miraya's arm. 'She's finishing up renovations at my place. You should come over and check out her work.'

'Is that true?' Anubhav's eyes widened with curiosity. 'Was that something you always wanted to do?'

Blushing, she nodded. 'Yes, I fought hard and earned a lucky break. My career took off after that.'

Leaning forward, he encouraged the conversation. 'What would it take to get your help, then?'

She laughed, setting her coffee down. 'Let's start with me seeing the place. Sometimes, when selling a house, a change in décor or paint can do wonders. I'll know how much to quote and we can sit down and discuss a budget.'

'So professional,' he breathed, leaning back in admiration. 'Where were you when I started my company?'

We all started laughing and I added, 'Indeed, Miraya is quite the handful to negotiate with.'

'So are you,' Miraya said, flustered, her cheeks red.

'Oh, we should go for a movie tomorrow,' Kasturi tugged at my sleeve, a gesture I looked forward to every time we went out now. 'You like to go on Fridays, right, Shaurya?'

'Y-yes,' I cupped my hand over hers and smiled wide. 'What about you, Anubhav? Do you like movies?'

He frowned and an expression of shame crossed his face. 'To be honest, I was so obsessed with my business, I never went.'

'Perfect,' Miraya gave him a warm smile. 'This can be something new in your new life.'

He returned the smile. 'You're right, Miraya. I would love to join you for a movie.'

'Excellent,' I clapped my hands. 'I'll get the tickets and we'll meet in front of the theatre. Just so you know, this is a weekly thing we try to do, Anubhav.'

'Sounds like something I can look forward to when

things get rough.' The tension had fallen away from Anubhav's shoulders for a change. 'I cannot thank you all enough for this. …'

'You don't have to thank us,' Kasturi patted his hand on the table. 'Just remember to choose life. Go after the things you want.'

'But, *what do I really want in life?*' Anubhav glanced at Miraya for a second before his eyes darted away. 'I'll have to give it some thought …' He wiped a tear off his cheek. The connection he and Miraya were creating with one another was just as special as the one I felt I had with Kasturi. I hoped they both could see that.

'Shaurya, you want to walk with me back to the hotel?' Anubhav had a lonesome look in his eyes. 'I'd rather have some company again, before being alone.'

I nodded; I couldn't say no, knowing he was still battling some demons. 'Absolutely. I am sure Kasturi and Miraya can make it home together.'

Smiling, Kasturi kissed my cheek. 'Thank you, Shaurya. You're so sweet.'

The heat from my cheeks made my eyes sting and Miraya hid her smile behind her hand. 'Anything to help …'

'If you need me, Anubhav, call me.' Miraya stood, spurring the rest of us to say our goodbyes. 'Be safe and see you soon.'

'Yes,' Anubhav said. 'I am a lucky man to have met you,

Miraya. I will admit that I'm terrified of the future, but I feel an odd sense of power now.'

'Perhaps making the decision to grasp hold of life can be a scary thing,' she responded, 'but that decision also emboldens you, nurtures you, pushes you forward. *That* is true power.'

'Do you think so?' he asked.

I nodded. 'Don't be too scared to face this fear head-on. The fear you feel is not meant to scare you; it's emerging to tell you how completely important this decision is for you.'

We went in opposite directions after leaving the café. The walk to the hotel was a silent one again. My eyes fell back to the bandages on his arm. Was his internal pain so deep that he had to cause himself external pain to forget about it? It made my stomach turn and I looked away. My thoughts wandered deeper into myself. Did I not still feel the sting of the incident in the railway station? Did it not hurt at the very core of my being when I thought of my inability to chase my dream or confess my feelings to Kasturi?

I hadn't even started the journey of chasing after my dream. Anubhav, on the other hand, had managed to make it come true and then ripped it away from himself. Perhaps those burns were reminders, punishment for the poor decisions from his past. My own struggles were small, meaningless, when I stood them beside what I had seen of

Anubhav's own. Why was it so hard? Anubhav was battling something far worse, and yet I felt as if I were dying every time I failed to go to Mumbai.

'I'm sorry about how the place was last time,' Anubhav's mumbling broke my thoughts and I found myself following him into the hotel room.

He pulled back the curtains, and sunlight flooded across the room. It still smelled of cigarettes; an ashtray next to a half-smoked pack of cigarettes sat on the table. Walking over to the nightstand, I picked up one of the two empty beer cans sitting there. We locked eyes and he frowned. Running his fingers through his hair, he slumped his shoulders in shame.

'I had a moment of weakness,' confessed Anubhav.

'Are there more?' I nodded at the mini-fridge.

He walked over to it and pulled out what was left of a six pack. 'I don't need the temptation here.'

I watched as he marched to the bathroom. One by one he popped them open and I listened to the glug-glug of the cans emptying out into the sink. As each can clanked into the trash can, Anubhav seemed to breathe easier. He needed the push I gave him, the stern reminder that alcohol was not his friend; I was a friend. Dropping the last empty can and the cardboard holder into the wastebasket, he smiled, leaning on the vanity. For once, the man Anubhav saw in the mirror was someone he felt confident and proud of being.

Sitting at the table, I flicked the pack of cigarettes against the ashtray. My lips parted to say something, but I stopped. He had managed a small victory with the beer. Ruining that with me nagging him over cigarettes seemed cruel. I smiled, also happy that Anubhav was trying hard to make changes for the better. Meeting three strangers at the cliffs of Amer Fort had been a good omen for him.

'Anubhav ...' I paused, waiting for him to come join me at the table. 'What does it feel like to have achieved your dream?'

'Freedom ... a sense of fulfilment ...' He leaned back in the chair and stared up at the ceiling. 'But recently there was a shadow over me, tinting the colour of my world. You have helped me chase that shadow away.

I took in the word *freedom*, realizing how tied down I felt on my current path. The empty frame on my wall was a prison cell for my soul. To live your dream was to be a free man; that was the truth. Anubhav gave it one word, a powerful word, and it stung hard against my heart and soul.

'What are you going to classes for?' He looked at me from the corner of his eye. 'I hear you have been studying hard, and I have been meaning to ask.'

'CA.' My reply was dry and bitter in tone.

He shifted in his chair, giving me his full attention. 'And that's not your dream?'

My mouth twisted in response, tight-lipped.

'What do you want to be doing?' His hands folded into one another on the table and I glared at them to avoid his eyes.

'What does it matter?' I flicked the cigarette pack again, annoyed to have started the conversation.

'It should matter a lot.' A sense of surprise came across his voice as he addressed me. 'Shaurya, I may not know what it is you really want to do, but the only person who can put you on that path is yourself. It takes devotion and a great deal of self-motivation to even start a dream career, goal, or path … whichever it may be for you.'

I braved looking him in the face and the sincerity in his eyes brought a weak smile from me.

'To reach for a dream, even if you are struggling, is the most freeing sensation in one's life.' His eyes dug deeper into my soul. 'Remember, only you are responsible from keeping yourself from achieving it. Don't let others' opinions and wants destroy that dream. It's what feels right in your heart.'

Covering my face with my palms, I mumbled, 'It feels so impossible with each passing day, Anubhav.'

'It will,' he agreed, his chair creaking under his shifting weight. 'In fact, it can feel like a mountain crashing down on you the longer you neglect it.'

Peeking between my fingers, I said, 'It does. I am buried under a mountain of regrets already.'

A grin crawled across his face, and he chuckled at the way I was pulling at my face. 'You'll reach a point where you have one final chance, Shaurya. When that moment happens, I hope you roll that mountain off your shoulder and take a step towards chasing after your dream. You're a good man; you deserve a life you are happy with.'

33

MIRAYA'S DIARY

I spoke to my parents again today. Sometimes I almost dread hearing their voices because I don't want to hear the pity that still seeps from their heart.

I am stronger now, though. Jaipur has been a healing city for me. As I venture out with my group of friends — Kasturi, Shaurya, and now Anubhav as well — I realize that not only is the city helping us heal, but it is also encouraging us to thrive.

With Anubhav in particular, every time we prowl around the beautiful buildings of this city, I notice the shadows around his eyes growing lighter and lighter.

He is still healing and I know that he still struggles with his vices, but I also know that their power over him is weakening each day.

As much as he is in my thoughts, I have only mentioned him to my parents for now. Their hopes were so dashed when my marriage ended, and I know their hearts broke for me as sharply as my own did. For now, Anubhav is a friend, someone our little group pulled back from the edge, literally and figuratively.

I keep thinking about his story. The agony he was in as he told it to us. It makes me angry that he was so ready to end that story, to cut it short. To tear the book of his life in half and plunk a 'the end' halfway through the telling.

Each day, every moment, our actions continue to write our story. In this document, our personas play out on stage, pushed and pulled by the events and encounters we have.

Without us stopping him, he would have taken that next half of his life story, the unwritten half, and thrown it away. He almost forced his unwritten story to remain unwritten.

But he didn't. He might have been scared of the instrument at first, but he has picked up the pen of life once again and is writing new paragraphs, new chapters, even now.

I think he realizes that he does control his life. He could not control his parents' accident, but he does have control over his own life. Every day, he experiences hundreds, maybe even thousands, of ways he can write his story.

Part of me wanted to champion his success when I spoke with my parents today, but not yet.

Perhaps another time we speak, I will tell them more about him. Because as much as my stomach jolts when our eyes meet, and I think perhaps he has some feelings for me too, I am not ready to think about that yet. This is only between you and me, my silent diary. I know you won't tell anyone.

34

SHAURYA

'I can't believe you hadn't brought Miraya here!' Anubhav was excited. 'Jantar Mantar has all sorts of architectural wonders, all centred around astronomy.'

'Really?' He had caught Miraya's attention.

The courtyard was filled with strange walls and stairs leading to nowhere. Some small, some large and all made with stunning skill. These were never intended to become buildings or even shelters, but instead were instruments. The masonry took my breath away, stone and bronze working together. Circles, sweeping swoops and hard angles could be seen in every device.

'I've been here a few times.' I peered over at Kasturi who looked more closely at one of the twelve structures we found ourselves lost between.

She looked back to me. 'What are these for then, Shaurya?'

Smiling, I recalled what I had learnt on my previous trips to the site. 'These are gnomon dials that measure the coordinates of stars, planets, and all twelve constellation systems. They track the position of the stars and depend on the earth's orbit around the sun more so than some of the others here.'

'Wow ...' Miraya was sketching some of the structures and shapes she found inspiring. 'And here I thought this was a mere collection of sundials.'

'Oh no, though we do have the largest,' chuckled Anubhav, peering over her shoulder to watch her work. 'Your artwork is inspiring. The way you see the world is beyond me, Miraya.'

'Thank you,' she said. 'Sometimes you can embrace art and use it as a way to travel without stepping a foot outside your home.'

'It's true,' Anubhav murmured, deep in thought. 'What a very unique perspective!'

She blushed. 'I draw inspiration from everywhere. Here I am seeing a connection between hard and soft angles that I've been wondering how to incorporate in some of my projects. It's like taking notes from those who came before me, or at times, from nature itself.'

'Really?' Anubhav's smile widened. 'Then we should walk you over to the Jai Prakash Yantra.'

'Oh, that might give you some great material, Miraya,'

I agreed. I had always loved the underground dome with its celestial markings and gaping dark rows between the marble slabs.

'I feel so guilty ...' Kasturi had returned to my side, her arm hooking through mine as she peered all around. 'I've been here a few times, but I can't remember what was designed to do what anymore.'

'It's okay. What Anubhav is referring to is the inverted map of the sky.' We were almost at the domes now. 'It's amazing to think this was all built centuries ago and, to this day, very accurate.'

'Amazing,' Miraya joined us to look down into the structure. 'What effort and soul must have been poured into this place, into each piece of stone.'

Anubhav took in her expression of awe before he spoke. 'The dream here was to be able to capture all the stars with the naked eye. See what could not be seen on a normal day.'

'They left behind quite the treasure.' Again, the pages of her sketchbook flipped open and her pencil went to work. 'The way each line in this place has a reason and purpose. Nothing fruitlessly placed. I can't get enough!'

'I am happy I was able to inspire you, Miraya.' Anubhav's words brought her pencil to a halt.

I watched as she bit her bottom lip. There was the familiar look of panic in her eyes before her shoulders slumped. Sighing, she sat up and turned to Anubhav.

Anubhav blinked, unsure as to what had brought the sudden shift in her body language. I knew why. It was hard to say if even Kasturi knew the depth of pain Miraya had experienced, but I had walked through her story. She might be looking to start again, but the sting of her past was still affecting her choices of the present. I held my breath as her lips parted, a look of sincerity on her face as she placed her hand on Anubhav's own.

'Anubhav ...' Her eyes fell away for few seconds before returning with the careful words she had picked. 'Please understand, it's very hard for me to feel close to anyone. My story has not been decided and well, you're a wonderful man. You should find a girl less ... broken than me.'

His own shoulders fell and he placed his other hand on top of hers now. 'I may not understand the pain you feel, Miraya. But for now, I am content with making you happy. More than anything, I want to see you inspired and as long as those eyes look forward, one day, you will know what sort of story you wish to write.'

Her lips twisted. 'Thank you for bringing me to this wonderful place.'

With that, she fell back into her artwork and Anubhav gave me a smile. He was happy with his new efforts in life, even if he could only sit and watch Miraya's own unfold.

'Shaurya,' Kasturi tugged my attention back to her. 'Do you know what that one is for?'

My eyes followed the direction she was pointing in as she pulled me to walk there. The large, looping walls of red, the stairs on either side and in the centre, were one of the more iconic attractions in the historical site. The white-bordered red walls called out for attention, but it was a mash-up of all of the things seen in the courtyard.

'That is Misra Yantra,' I said as we came to a stop beside it.

She broke away from me, taking in the structure. 'What on earth does this one do?'

Rubbing my jaw, I searched my memories for an answer. 'Hmm, all I really remember is it's actually five astronomical tools in one. I can only assume a sundial is one of those five.'

She laughed. 'Really, Shaurya? You don't know?'

Shaking my head, I chuckled. 'I am not a scientist, nor an astronomer. This looks as alien to me as it does to you.'

I followed her as she circled the building, leaving the watchful eyes of Miraya and Anubhav. We were still giggling and my bravery swelled in me, like the flickering of a flame on the wick of a candle. It would have been a perfect time to confess to Kasturi that I liked her — to say those words or even ask her out or to be my girlfriend. But like a candle in the wind, the words were blown out as soon as I opened my mouth. I stopped, looking to the ground in shame; my soul feeling betrayed by my doubts and fears.

'Shaurya?' Her voice was worried and I looked up, mustering a half-smile. 'Is something wrong?'

I shook my head and lied. 'I'm fine, just a lot on my mind.'

'Oh, that's right.' She skipped back closer to me. 'You have your CA finals coming soon.'

The fact ripped through my heart like a knife, rendering me speechless.

'Don't worry.' Her hands gripped my shoulders and her expression filled with hope. 'I need to study for my own exams. We can encourage one another to work hard.'

Still no words came to my lips, so I nodded my agreement.

'Miraya and Anubhav can keep one another company.' She took my hand, leading us back towards where Miraya was shutting her book again. 'Miraya!'

My eyes caught Miraya's own and I could see that she sensed the pain I was feeling. Her mouth twisted and she turned to give us her full attention. Anubhav was wiping sweat from his brow, but my expression made even him flinch. Was I so obvious? Could Kasturi see it yet not express it to me?

'This will be our last outing.' Her hand tightened on mine and my heart was startled for a breath or two. 'Shaurya and I will have to focus this next week to prepare for finals.'

Miraya nodded and looked to me with a stern expression. 'So it's that close, the CA finals?'

'Y-yes.' Her face echoed the sensation the empty frame on my wall gave me. 'So perhaps Anubhav can take you out to some of the other sights Jaipur offers.'

My voice came out dry, but Anubhav's eyes sparkled. 'Yes, it would be a pleasure to do that.'

Miraya grimaced, but shook herself from it. 'Sure. After all, Anubhav picked this place, and it's been a great reference to build on for future projects.'

'Excellent.' Kasturi's stomach grumbled then and she blushed. 'Anyone ready for lunch?'

'There are no words to express how cute that is ...' I couldn't contain my grin as I squeezed her hand. 'Yes, let's go have lunch.'

'I know a great place near here,' Anubhav said. 'And they have wonderful teas and coffee.'

'Coffee sounds amazing right now,' confessed Miraya.

35

MIRAYA'S DIARY

Kasturi and Shaurya have been busy with studies of late. I have taken it upon myself to be Anubhav's guiding light in the meantime. I am rather proud of his efforts these last few weeks. He has finally let go of the drinking.

I think part of it is that, as we meet and talk, we share more of our past with one another. Both of us have been through so much. Dreams coming true, while other dreams were ripped away. It's as if we take turns wiping the tears of pain from our cheeks. Voices shaken by the agony we shared with one another. I haven't felt this close to someone in a long time. ...

Is it because I saved Anubhav?

This overwhelming sense of responsibility to help him in his new life is a weight I am more than happy to carry. I sometimes feel as if he is giving me the chance to start my life over again. Regardless, we are both learning you can't heal or move on alone. It takes the care and affection of other people in your life to keep you from the edge.

The way he describes his parents, I can't help but see my own. They were loving and encouraging. More importantly, much like my own, thrilled to hear he had succeeded. My heart aches to know they were on their way to see him. He had been so busy with the business's growing success, it was going to be the first time he was seeing them since he left Jaipur. I would imagine this left him with a massive sense of guilt.

If it were me, I would be stuck in a never-ending loop of I should have seen them sooner or If I had gone to them this would never had happened! The anger he must have felt towards himself was what drove him to drink. Worse, the drunken state he found himself in at their funeral was fuel to the fire.

Chills rattle me to imagine sitting in my parents' house knowing they were gone. I want to help him through this. He is doing his best to start a new life, and one way for him to move on is to leave behind the last remnants of his parents by selling the home they left him. I can do that. With my talent and resolve, I want to do that for him.

I was floored to hear about his skills as a businessman and the clever ways he organized it. He's so smart, and to think he couldn't pull himself out of his depression. I think I will ask him more about running a business. At the moment, since I left Mumbai behind, I am freelancing. Deep down, I really want to start my own firm, and maybe this is a chance for Anubhav to start again. He seems to miss having a company, and it shows regret is still haunting him over the whole failure of keeping that much of his past life intact.

Shaurya still hasn't confessed to Kasturi that he likes her. The two of them have been studying together, their bond growing. I wonder if he will be able to write that next chapter.

Is life only a game of yes or no? I wonder about the absolutes that we try to create for ourselves; our relationships, our life choices. We try to make things black and white, when sometimes it's much more grey.

I think I am falling for Anubhav.

It's funny; I don't get the idea of 'falling in love'. From day one, I've only seen myself rising higher and higher, floating on love, not falling under it.

My feelings for Anubhav excite me and terrify me at the same time. I don't want to love again. But my heart seems to have other opinions.

We went to the movies, and the swelling in my heart when he reached over and held my hand was almost too much. I see it in his eyes and body too. The way he leans in when I speak and the smiles we exchange. Often my heart races and my palms go sweaty. It's like a phantom from my past, but it's not the face I saw when I last experienced this. I'm not ready. I don't want to hurt Anubhav either.

For now, I do what I can to mention how unready I am for a relationship. Constant reminders to him of how I still feel the sting of my divorce in my soul and heart; when I say it, his eyes tell me he is willing to wait for the time when I am ready. I wonder if I will be ready, ever.

36

SHAURYA

I couldn't sleep. The final exams were coming closer, like an arranged meeting with Death himself. My soul ached and my thoughts hissed at night. My eyes kept falling on that empty frame and my stomach would turn. Was I really giving up on this dream? Anger seeped into me like a burning heat.

Where was my courage?

I needed it!

The one thing that was going right for me was the time I was spending with Kasturi. She was preparing for her own exams and we had decided to study together. Watching her serious face as she read and took notes, my mind would trail off. The way her braid fell down one shoulder, and her lips curved. She was so beautiful, and I was nothing more than a coward.

Miraya's words bit at my mind when I looked at Kasturi.

When would I change my story, fix it with that first step and confess to her how much I liked her. No, it was as Miraya had said: *I love her.* There was no denying it with each silent session, sitting side by side with our books. The difference was, she was studying and I was not. My eyes would look down at the letters and words on the pages in the book in my hands. But not even the word '*the*' was legible to me.

And then there was the thought of that empty frame.

Every step I took closer to the final exams, my soul twisted into tighter knots, leaving my heart aching for the dream I was leaving behind. Then again, if I couldn't focus on studying, how was I supposed to pass the exams? There was still no guarantee I would make it through these exams.

'Shaurya.' Kasturi's voice jolted me from my out-of-focus gaze on my book. 'Are you feeling well?'

'Y-yes,' I nodded, mustering a fake smile. 'Just nervous about the final exams; running out of time at this rate.'

'But …' Her eyes fell to my notebook where I was holding a pen hostage. 'You haven't written down anything for the last two days.'

My face flushed and, looking down, I could see she was right. For the last two days I had simply held my pen ready to write, but nothing had been done. If she could see the notes before this page, she would laugh. They weren't informative at all. In fact, I had ripped one out and trashed it when I realized I had gone from notes on a subject to my own panicked thoughts.

'Ha …' Setting everything off to the side, I rubbed my face with my hands, hiding it from her. 'I think I've been pushing myself too hard lately.'

The warmth of her hand rubbing my back sent my heartbeat speeding. 'Why don't you take a nap or go get some coffee?'

My cheeks held a heat in them and I sighed, 'I think a nap might do me some good.'

I left Kasturi behind on the terrace with a heavy heart. So many thoughts were plaguing me. Feelings from all different angles were colliding into a tangled ball at my core, and there were no signs of where I could start to break the knot apart. I hated ending a moment with Kasturi. What was I doing? What did I want to do?

'Shaurya?' The voice from the kitchen called out to me.

I had closed the door harder than normal, absent-minded with the weight of my plight. 'Yes, it's me.'

'Can you come grab something off the top shelf for me please?' From the sound of her voice, Mom was flustered.

Walking into the kitchen, I saw she had her sleeves rolled up and was working some spices into a mixture in a massive bowl. The smell was sharp in my nostrils and rich enough to make my stomach grumble. It was one of my favourite curry blends which she used in a lot of the recipes that she cooked. I pointed to a canister at the top of the only open cabinet and she nodded. Placing it on the counter, I leaned over her shoulder to take in the wonderful amalgamation of ingredients happening.

'Do you always knead it this much?' I asked.

'Absolutely.' She was standing on a step-stool so she could reach inside the bowl to put weight into her actions. 'It's the only way to blend the spices and herbs evenly.'

'What did you need the other canister for?' I lifted an eyebrow at the mysterious metal tin with no labels. 'It doesn't even say what it is …'

'That's the secret ingredient.' Looking over her shoulder, she gave me a coy smile. 'That there is the real deal-maker for the flavour in most of my cooking.'

'Oh yeah?' I picked it up and opened the canister, only to have my senses overwhelmed. 'It's strong … what on earth is it?'

Chuckling, she shook her head. 'When you get married, I'll tell your wife.'

I closed it, fussing at her, 'It'll be a long time before I find out then. Did I smell nutmeg in that?'

'Maybe.' She lifted an eyebrow, still working the bowl.

'So there's more than one spice?' I lifted my own eyebrow in response.

'Perhaps.' Laughing, she looked about the counter. 'Ugh, where is the jar of rice.'

'Up here.' I pulled it from the cabinet and set it next to the bowl.

'What would I do without you here, Shaurya?' She started rinsing her hands in the sink beside me. 'I wouldn't be able to reach half the kitchen ...'

I laughed, shaking my head. 'You would just need a taller step-stool, Mom.'

37

ANUBHAV

'Where on earth are you taking me?' Miraya asked suspiciously. The taxi ride was taking longer than she had anticipated.

'A fairly new place in Jaipur, but I think you will enjoy the tour and dinner I have planned.' My heart was racing, both from excitement and fear that I had upset her. 'I let them know an interior designer was interested in seeing the resort.'

'Resort?' She lifted an eyebrow. 'Dinner?'

Waving my hand in defence, I reassured her. 'We're not staying the night! Trust me, when we get out of the car, you'll fall in love with the place.'

Relief washed over me when the taxi took a turn into the last stretch leading up to the resort. Without Shaurya or Kasturi present, Miraya had proved to be edgy and uncomfortable. That she had come along at all, considering the tension building in the taxi, was a light at the end of a tunnel for me. She had saved my life, after all. The man who swore to protect and love her forever had hurt her so deeply. If I could mend even a fraction of that part of her life, I would die a happy man. How could he have not been proud to be the husband of someone so strong?

The taxi rolled to a stop and I rushed out eagerly to open her door for her. She stepped out and the look of worry on her face rattled me. Looking over my shoulder, I smiled. Everywhere was greenery and it would seem at first that we had been dropped off in a jungle. Laughing at her expression, I pointed to the green sign by the walkway that read, *The Treehouse Resort.* Her eyes widened and I earned the first smile since we had started the drive. She ventured down the pathway and I paid the taxi his due.

'I have heard of this place!' she said, a hand to her chest as she started to take in the surroundings. 'I didn't realize it was in Jaipur!'

Smiling, I nodded. 'I figured that had to be the case. I'm sure in your studies it came up at least once, right?'

'Yes, in fact, a few times.' There was a twinkle in her eyes as she turned one way and then the other. 'And you said we were taking a tour?'

'That's right.'

She gripped my hand and my heart swelled. 'Oh, Anubhav ...' Now she was tugging me along, eager to see the inside of the resort. 'You're amazing!'

The path to the lobby was beautiful. Flowering vegetation gathered at the base of towering trees leaning high above. Peering out from between the plants were various statues of Hindu gods. Miraya stopped, her eyes locked on one as she opened her sketchbook to capture what her eyes and mind saw. I waited, silent with my admiration of her talent. The gentle chirps of birds echoed through the leaves as a breeze blew past.

I had brought her here in the hope of giving her a few moments of peace and serenity. The turmoil she had been scarred with still bothered me. No longer was I concerned with my own failures and fall from grace. The only thing I wanted was to help Miraya overcome her pain, encourage her to start her life again as she had asked me to do with my own. A million *thank you*s would never make up for saving me back at Amer Fort. Satisfied she had captured what she wanted, we finished our walk. Reaching the lobby at last, a smile on her face, I approached the front desk.

'My name's Anubhav,' I said. I looked over my shoulder and watched as Miraya took in every detail, her pencil never resting as it scribbled across the page. 'I have an arrangement for a tour and reservations later at the Peacock Bar.'

'Ah, yes!' The girl picked up the phone and dialled an extension number. 'Your private tour guests are here. Yes, yes, ma'am. Mr. Anubhav, she'll be right out.'

After a few minutes, a formally-dressed woman came out, hand stretched out to shake mine. 'My brother has told me much about you, Anubhav. I am glad to see your health is improving!'

'Th-thank you.' Blushing, I waved Miraya over. 'Miraya, this is Tamanna. She's one of the main marketers for the resort and sister to a business colleague of mine.'

'Oh, hello.' They shook hands, firm and professional in the movements. 'I'm an interior designer —'

'— from Mumbai.' Tamanna smiled. 'You actually did work for another client I know of, and I have to say, you worked wonders in their place.'

Miraya's shoulders relaxed and she took on a more confident tone. 'I am happy to hear my reputation is spreading so far.'

'Indeed.' Motioning for us to follow, Tamanna lead the way. 'If you have some suggestions for anything here or if like what you see, I would love your input.'

'Absolutely.' The smile on Miraya's face was everything I was hoping for.

We followed close behind Tamanna through all the places the resort had to offer. We stood in awe next to the waterfall feature where a wall of water cascaded down rocks. The head of a statue had been placed in just the right place to bring the eyes to the centre of the water feature, a divine sensation. Leaning over Miraya's shoulder, Tamanna and

I watched as she sketched out one of the parrots, labelling the colours with names I could only assume existed in her palettes of pencils and paints back home. Tamanna was impressed, and enjoying the tour as much as we were.

We moved on then, and as we walked we saw, in the distance, a tree-house taking shape. Climbing up to the entry, Tamanna unlocked the door and let us in. Miraya gasped, stunned by the ambience within. Earthen elements were cleverly mixed with a contemporary styling and layout. Moreover, the abstraction of the branches snaking through the room here and there made for a surreal sensation. Miraya's fingers ran across the bark of the tree, making sure this was indeed a tangible item within the living space.

'This is incredible.' She wandered around the room, marvelling over the branches cutting through even the bathroom. 'I love how the branches completely break the clean, contemporary layout.'

Miraya began working in her sketchbook, writing notes to herself. 'In fact, seeing it in person changes my initial thoughts. It's a reminder that I am in a tree-house, but the untouched element of it makes me feel like I am still outside in a way.'

'We want our guests to feel connected to nature, yet also enjoy the luxury aspect of being in a resort,' Tamanna explained, while she waited patiently at the door for Miraya to finish her observations. 'The goal was to keep with earth tones and elements for the décor, to soften the disruption of the branches growing through the rooms.'

'But I love the disruption,' Miraya said, laughing as her thoughts rushed forward. 'It makes you think the tree grew through the building, not that the tree-house was built around the tree.'

I laughed too, flipping my perspective to match the notion. 'I see what you mean! Like the tree cut through like lightning.'

'Yes!'

We left the tree-house behind and walked with Tamanna back towards the Peacock Bar. The sun was starting to fall into the evening sky. The clouds, painted in shades of yellow and orange, were like a spectrum of saffron one could almost taste in the air. We rounded another turn and worked our way higher until we finally reached the last stop of the night. Tamanna said her goodbyes and wished us an excellent evening.

'This is … wow …' Miraya took a seat, marvelling over the carved building and spectacle before her.

Wooden peacocks stood guard within columns etched with patterns of foliage. The arches of the doorways and windows were carved with skill, the tinier dips and curves reflected in them all. I glanced at Miraya's face, and the elation and stunned look on it was priceless. This would be a memory I would treasure for a long time, and I hoped she felt the same.

After half an hour, she dared to attempt to sketch some of the patterns and borders that made up the tinier banners carved on either side of the doorway. It was the first time I saw her challenged while replicating and recording what lay before her. Several times she took her eraser to the paper, walking to another angle, sometimes closer, sometime further. She smiled at times; at times shook her head in dismay.

'Is it that complex? And why don't you simply click pictures instead of sketching?' I asked, fascinated by her attempt to capture the shrine-like building.

'I want to feel the art; I want to feel the thought-process of the original artist who created it. I want to feel the making of it. Only then can I learn from it. And so I don't take photographs; I sketch.'

She tapped the end of her pencil on her lips for a minute before finishing her words. 'It amazes me how the patterns evolve at different angles and distances. I am floored by the artist's miraculous skill in carving. No painting in a million years could hope to achieve what blossoms here before my eyes in wood.'

Taking her words to heart, I found myself shifting where I stood; right then left, closer and the back again. 'It's like infinity brought to life.'

'Indeed ...' The pencil now tapped her cheek. 'I have to sketch the same section three or four times to capture all the intricate elements. What a fascinating piece hidden here … no one ever talks about this part …'

'A lot of people overlook the relics and artwork from the past.' I smiled to myself before making my claim: 'So did I finally find something Miraya's hands can't duplicate?'

She glared at me, rolling her eyes. 'You have only challenged me.'

'Ah …' my eyebrows lifted high. 'Are you hungry yet?'

The thought was enough to send her stomach grumbling. 'Oh my, Kasturi's rubbing off on me … or at least my tummy.'

Laughing, I took her hand and led her to where I had arranged for us to eat dinner. The sun had fallen deeper in the sky, the saffron now turning purple above our heads. Shadows were dancing with the wavering of candles and lanterns and the food was both artistic and delicious. With each passing second, seeing the smile I was able to create on Miraya's face, the more my heart yearned for her. The way she covered her lips with her elegant fingers to hide her grins. A flush of red would hit her cheeks and her eyes would fall away from mine with every compliment I paid her work. I couldn't get enough.

'I have to be honest, Anubhav.' Her laughter fell away and she took on a more serious tone and look. 'I was afraid this was your way of ensnaring me to go on a date after I said no.'

Shaking my head, I gave a meek smile. 'I wanted to bring you someplace special, to inspire you some more.'

'Thank you.'

'No, Miraya, thank you.' A waiter took away our plates, leaving us alone with the candle at the table. 'Thanks to you I am giving life a second chance.'

'You and I hold the power to change our lives,' she said. Again, the wonderful blush and the cupping of her hand to cover it. 'Every story deserves a rewrite I suppose …'

'This is my story and I want to write the best one. But I cannot write it without you. You know why? Because …' Tears were filling my eyes, the words flooding out of me with all my heart and soul. 'I love you, Miraya.'

Her eyes grew wide, the fingers hiding the lips. I couldn't see those rosebud folds, but the sparkle deep in her eyes was enough to let me know she felt those words.

'You made me the man I am today. You taught me how to live, how to love, how to laugh, how to hope,' I whispered. 'I find myself in your voice, your laughter. You have made me a better man.'

'I was only there to help you remember life is worth living,' she insisted.

'And you have. I hope someday that my story can be written with yours. It is my deepest wish right now.'

Miraya's eyes suddenly flooded with tears. 'Thank you,' she whispered. 'I'm just —'

I couldn't let her put voice to her doubts, and I needed to reassure her that I didn't expect her feelings to be returned. Not yet. I continued quickly before I lost my courage. 'I don't know from where you came into my life and where you'll fly one day. I just know that you are the most beautiful gift I ever received and time spent with you is just awesome. It's all that I can ever wish for.'

'My time with you has been amazing as well. You have taught me how valuable life is. I confess to being confused now. You have surprised me tonight.'

'I surprised myself,' I admitted. 'I didn't mean to fall in love with you, but I find now that my thoughts end in your eyes. I can lie. But my eyes and my heart will never allow me to do so.' And with my eyes, I searched deep in hers, seeing confusion, hope, excitement and a trickling stream of sadness in there.

I continued, 'I will wait for when you are ready. I just wanted you to know that, with every passing day, I realize how much you mean to me.' Wiping the tears away before they could fall, I gestured to a waiter for our bill. 'It's been a long day, after all.'

She nodded, closing her eyes tight as a single tear fell. The ride home was silent, but the tension from before was nowhere to be found. I had done everything I could to express my affection for her and what made her who she was. Only time would prove how deep my words had struck into her soul and broken heart.

38

Miraya's Diary

Anubhav spoke the most amazing words that have ever graced my ears.

'This is my story and I want to write the best one. But I cannot write it without you. You know why? Because ... I love you, Miraya.'

The whole world froze in that moment. I was swallowed by a torrent of emotions: happiness, terror, even confusion. My face gave me away; his smile slipped when I told him it was unexpected. I've known he liked me and have tried so hard to deter him, but this ... I didn't expect the feelings I would have in this matter.

Yes, I need time to take this in, though it's been a few days since he said it. I am only writing now, since I don't know what to think or feel. My confusion is a mixture of excitement and fear over the words he said to me. And surprise too, over how happy I was to hear them. I didn't want to fall in love again! My pain from ... it still hurts! But at some point, I realized that no matter how hard I try, I can't keep running from my own self, my own soul.

And I got the answers. What I need is not to escape from my own self, but to change my thinking/thoughts.

I want to let myself fall in love, or better, rise in love. That much I have realized in this moment of my own story. Yet, deep down I am scared and not ready to go back down that path. Anubhav, I don't want to hurt you or drive you away. If anyone understands my pain, and me, it is you.

Back and forth I pace, both inside myself and on this terrace, looking for an answer. What should I say to him?

My fear of pushing Anubhav away and hurting him is much greater than the reluctance to consider loving someone. I don't think I'm ready for a relationship, though being loved is something that I do want. For now, I pray he understands I need time. These wounds from my divorce still feel like they are bleeding. Even the slap on my face that forced me to file my divorce still stings on my cheek.

I hope Anubhav understands …

I hope he can wait for me …

I always considered myself, my actions, to be medicine. I have only ever wanted to help. Mohit made me feel like I was a poison for him. My own dreams put a bitter taste on his tongue. I blamed myself for the longest time, but now I realize I was not a dangerous pill — it was he who forced my perspective to change. I let him twist my goodness, but that was his negativity.

I was, and am now, a creator, not a destroyer.

Yes, I would love to be with Anubhav. We share a painful past and were both broken. Unlike Mohit, I do not see a jealous man in Anubhav. I am not competition to him; in fact, he admires and encourages success in a business. He is capable of appreciating my dream and I would love to rekindle his own dream. We are both struggling to write new stories and we are both pushing through our doubts.

He is trying so hard to stay sober, to break his habit of smoking, and I cannot help but feel it is only possible through his newfound love for me. This man does not see me as a trophy, but a woman who deserves a man who respects and cares for her. Without him, I would not be reconsidering my own views of love again.

When we are together, I feel afraid and excited, and it has been a very long time since I felt this way. Marriage is still a bridge I am not willing to see in my future, but allowing someone to love me, and loving them back, that I should be able to do. After denying myself it, I miss it, I crave it, but it terrifies me. With Anubhav, I am safe; I know he would harm himself before ever lifting a hand on me. He is a gentle man, and though it may be his flaw, it is also his strongest point.

39

SHAURYA

Splashing my face with cool water, I did my best to get back focus. May was extremely hot, the pressure of the sun and the responsibilities fast approaching were suffocating me. I had my finals the following week, and it was difficult to think about them without a flood of emotions rattling through me. The invisible chains on the bench in the railway station were gentle in comparison to the phantom claws digging inside me. It was unclear as to whether the feelings were clawing to get in or come out of me. Frustrated, staring into my own eyes in the bathroom mirror, I had no words for the emotions tearing me apart.

Breaking away, ashamed of who I saw there, I marched to the terrace for some fresh air. Rounding the corner, I smiled to see Miraya there, writing in her diary. She paused, closing the book on her lap. I waved and she motioned for me to sit by her.

'Hello, Miraya.' Sitting, I stretched, trying to wake myself further. 'How are you doing?'

'Conflicted,' her fingers rolled into her palms, fist pressing against her diary. 'About a lot of things in my life ...'

My eyes widened with curiosity to hear more. 'And what brought on this new wave of conflict? It wasn't something I did, was it?'

'No,' she laughed before her face fell back to the stern expression. 'Anubhav confessed he loves me.'

My eyebrows lifted high as I took in the information. 'Wow.'

She nodded. 'Wow is one way of putting it.'

'How does that make you feel, Miraya?' I watched as her fists tightened.

'I am scared.' She turned and her eyes were fierce. 'To be honest, I didn't want love in my life anymore.'

'And now?'

'I am conflicted.'

'Give yourself a second chance to love, Miraya.' My words flowed from me before I could stop them. 'You deserve to be loved.'

'And what about you, Shaurya?' There was an aggressive tone in her reply. 'When will you let yourself love? What if there isn't a second chance?'

The words sent my heart racing and I was speechless.

'Should I tell Kasturi?' she offered.

'No ...' I tried to turn the topic back to her. 'But, Miraya, you should really think about yourself. What do you want ...'

'And you should think about yourself, Shaurya,' she smiled. 'I would never tell Kasturi. It is up to you to win her love. No one can ever do that for you and it doesn't always wait for you. So, Shaurya, look deep in yourself and decide what you want and take action.'

She walked away, leaving me there confused. Miraya had managed to take her internal conflict and pass it to me, but then again, I had come here already struggling with myself. I couldn't figure out what it was I wanted more in my life. What was it that I wanted for myself? Not what my parents or peers had pushed on me, but deep down, what did I want for myself at this very moment?

I had to try one last time. If I could only make my dad understand ...

Across the dinner table later that evening, I sat in despondent silence with my mom and dad, feeling the desire to talk about my dream draining out of my spirit, like a great presence was pushing the energy out of my body.

I was in the same situation as I had been four years ago, asking the same question, but hoping for a different answer this time. It had taken me years to find this courage again, and now, perhaps, it was my last chance.

Suddenly, the energy resurged.

'I want to quit CA and go to Mumbai to be a filmmaker,' I said in a low but firm voice.

My dad was shocked to hear about my dream again after so many years.

'What are you talking about? Have you gone mad? You have your final exams next week and you want to quit CA? Are you in your senses?' He banged the table furiously.

'Dad, I really want to do this. There are a lot of people who truly think I can make it in the industry.' I leaned forward in my chair, desperate to make him realize how much this meant to me. 'My friends, my teachers, they have all seen my work. Many think this is a good step for me.'

My dad snorted. 'They would encourage you to chase this silly dream ... even if you fail?'

'But they do not see me failing. They see me succeeding!'

'How can they know this?' my mom responded. 'Do they know a lot of famous filmmakers?'

I felt myself growing angry but I pushed it down. Losing my temper was not a good idea. But as I pushed away the anger, I felt my resolve breaking again.

'No, they do not,' I admitted. 'But they see in me talent and passion. Please, just let me go. I can do this.'

My dad shook his head. 'No, son. Your place is here, not off chasing your dreams. It's too much of a risk. You're young still; some day, you'll thank me for urging you to be careful with your future. Just go back to your room now and study.'

40

Miraya's Diary

It's hard to believe I go back to Mumbai tomorrow.

My time here in Jaipur has been an incredible journey. Over the last three months, Destiny has taught me so much about friendship, dreams, life, and love. And now, I must make a decision.

Should I accept Anubhav in my life?

He loves me, I know this. And I want to let myself love him too.

But he has had so much disappointment in his life — what if we don't work out? What if our story together was never meant to be written?

Facing my return to Mumbai, I can't help but think about how my dreams slowly dissolved until they finally shattered with the slap on my face.

A relationship may work on some soothing lies. But it lasts only on truths. Even if the truth is difficult, a healthy relationship would be able to take it, and only become stronger. Lies will only make shallow the essence of a relationship.

I know Anubhav is not Mohit. Mohit worked to destroy my story; Anubhav wants to write his with mine. He wants us to work together and draw strength from our love.

But can my heart allow it?

To give love in my life a second chance and risk breaking what is left of my heart and soul? Or should I stand firm on what I had decided, that no more would I welcome love in my life?

I started to make for myself a new life, a new story, much like Anubhav and Shaurya have. Their words, their struggles have spoken to me in ways words cannot express. What do I want my story to be when I step foot off the train in Mumbai?

Sometimes, always is not enough. Can it be for us?

41

MIRAYA'S DIARY

It's been haunting me for days now, but I have decided.

I cannot imagine being in Mumbai, facing the phantoms of my past, without a hand to hold. Anubhav will be coming to Mumbai with me and together we will continue to write a new story. We both have scars in our hearts, but we don't want to give up on life and I have decided I do not want to give up on love.

Anubhav is a genius at business. Together we will forge a story that intertwines both our dreams into one. Perhaps this was where Mohit and I went wrong. … He was living his dream, he made my own possible, and instead of holding on to one another, we let ourselves be pulled apart. I will continue to do what I love so much and Anubhav will get his second chance to start a business. I'm still in a state of being excited and nervous, but I no longer fear going back to Mumbai.

Yes, I was so afraid my time here in Jaipur was coming to an end, but that has washed away knowing Anubhav will be by my side. Only time will decide how much more I can let myself accept love ... but Anubhav is understanding and is beyond patient with me.

And I suppose I am patient with him. He still struggles; these days it's a cigarette here and there when his stress gets to him. The drinking has stopped completely. Even when he's offered one, he's learned to say no. Often he seeks me in these moments, squeezing my hand tight to hold on to the railing. I wonder if he realizes he's often the armour I've been needing to brave the monster I had labelled as love. He must know.

It is funny how this all came about thanks to Shaurya. His words echo constantly in my heart: Give life a second chance and write a new story. Yet, I watch him tie himself further down a path of a life he has no faith in, leaving behind his dreams. If I can do anything for him before I leave for Mumbai, I hope I can make him see that he is far braver than he could ever know.

Shaurya helped me reconsider love, he pulled Anubhav back from death, and he inspires Kasturi to study hard. Though he fears disappointing his parents, and feels obligated to pursue a career as a CA because that is what is expected of him, it is clear it will never make him happy. He has given courage to all of us, but will he ever have it for his own self? Will he ever justify the meaning of his name?

42

SHAURYA

I found myself glaring at the flashing lights in the railway station. Kasturi grabbed my hand, pulling me past the vendors and crowds of people waiting for their trains. The last time I had braved walking down this path, I had been alone. Looking over my shoulder, I saw we had passed the sign pointing towards Platform No. 2. Swivelling my head, I found the bench I often chained my soul to, and a pang struck my heart.

Again, the smell of various foods mixed with the grease and grime of the trains. Shouts and rumblings of people in the station couldn't reach my thoughts. Instead, I saw the falling papers and the sorrow-filled eyes of the man who asked, *Are you coming?*

A train whizzed past, picking up some trash and flinging it to the air. It was as if one last snowflake from my last failure had come to laugh at me. I bit my bottom lip, a sour taste on my tongue filled with angry words. I shook the feeling away. I was here to say goodbye to some new and marvellous friends and not lament over a failed past.

Miraya and Anubhav were standing next to the bench with their luggage. I could hear my blood rushing through my ears as I stumbled to a stop, staring out towards the tracks. The man's words came back to me: *If you don't give all of yourself to the life you want, heart, soul and mind, you won't go anywhere at all …*

'Shaurya?' Kasturi's voice reached me on the third try. 'Are you okay?'

I nodded, not wanting to answer her in a shaken voice and cause unwanted alarm.

Miraya laughed. 'That's right, last time we were here you had that same look on your face.'

'We?' Kasturi asked, puzzled. She hadn't heard the story. 'You were here, Shaurya?'

Swallowing, I confessed, 'I came here to spend some time with myself; I hadn't realized Miraya was here as well.'

It was a small lie, but how could I tell someone I cared so much for about the number of times I'd planned to run away from here and from her? Regardless, Miraya was kind enough to allow me to be the one to relate my own failures to her.

'Some man knocked into me, and my sketches flew everywhere.' She made a big motion with both her arms, able to laugh over the event now. 'They came raining down all over the platform! Scurrying away like feral kittens running away from me, darting from one end to the other.'

'It was like snow ...' Shaking my head, I squinted with embarrassment. 'And I was terrible. I didn't lift a finger to help. ... I can never forgive myself knowing that ... if I had known ...'

Miraya smiled. 'But when someone is struggling to write their story, it's hard to see what's happening around you.'

My eyes opened and her forgiveness shone brightly, breaking the phantom of that day for me. It rolled over me and I was able to breathe again, a smile coming forward. Miraya was trying to replace it with a reminder of the words she had shouted to me back on the terrace, *If you are brave enough to get to the station, why don't you let yourself follow through?*

As if reading my mind, Miraya said softly, 'There are opportunities that come and go, like the trains on this very track. You can climb on any train and it will take you down a new path. But you need to decide which platform to stand on and which train is the one that is the most important for you.'

I thought about her words. *Life is always presenting new opportunities. I may not have taken the chance before, but that doesn't mean I have missed that opportunity, right? It's time to be brave and grab hold of that second chance.*

Brave. My heart suddenly started beating as if it were trying to jump out of my chest. 'Kasturi, I need to speak with you,' I said abruptly, glancing down the tracks. The train was not in sight. I still had time.

She giggled a little at my urgency. 'You're speaking with me now, silly,' she teased.

Without responding, I grabbed her hand and whisked her to the nearest bench. Now her smile was gone, replaced with confusion.

My heart thudding, I thought about being in my parents' dining room. Garnering my courage to tell them my dreams. Twice. Would Kasturi crush this dream as my parents had driven my dream of Mumbai into the ground?

No, I thought. *This is different. Kasturi would never do that to me.*

'Kasturi … I … I love you,' I blurted out and watched her reel back as she took in this new truth.

'I don't understand,' she said slowly.

'I love you,' I repeated. *Can't you come up with more than that?* my mind cajoled.

'How? Why?'

I grinned. 'The moment I started asking myself "why", I started getting answers. Life is worth only in the moments lived with you.'

'It is?' she asked breathlessly.

I grasped her hand; it was shaking, despite the heat.

'Do you feel the same way? Please tell me you do,' I said in a rush.

Her lips curved slowly into a radiant smile, as tears of happiness fell down her face and caught on that perfect smile.

'I do,' she said simply.

Hearing those words, I wanted to throw my entire being around her and wrap her in the most loving embrace, never to let go. Instead, I gently cupped her face in my hands, brushed the salty tears from her lips and settled for the most magical kiss of my life.

'Oh,' I moaned happily. 'I have always wanted to kiss you. I wanted to read you. I wanted to talk to your soul.'

She lay her head on my shoulder and sighed. 'I have dreamed of this moment,' she said. 'But now it's time to bid goodbye to our friends.'

Dropping a soft kiss once more on my lips, she stood, squared her shoulders and pulled me back to my feet.

As we rejoined our friends, our fingers laced in each other's, Miraya grinned happily. 'Some stories are hidden deep within you,' she said, pulling Kasturi and me into a warm embrace. 'You just need to find them.'

'You always speak such great truths, Miraya,' Anubhav said, smiling as he picked up their bags. 'The train is pulling in, now's your chance to say goodbye. It won't wait long, they never do.'

My eyes jerked to the incoming train wobbling down the tracks. People were shifting along with us, grabbing their things, eager to move on from this place. Miraya and Kasturi hugged each other tight and my heart leaped into my throat.

Could I really go? Should I stay? Why was I feeling this way? My future was set, finals so close, and my dreams snuffed out. My future was empty as the frame on the wall, but with my parents happy, I was where I should be, wasn't I? Where was this burning in my soul coming from? Was this my last chance? Was this where my story would end?

'Thank you for all the hard work in my room!' Tears were falling from Kasturi's eyes, painting the back of Miraya's shirt.

'You're welcome, my dear!' She turned, grabbing their last bag as the train screeched to a stop. 'Mumbai, here I come!'

'Thank you, Shaurya,' Anubhav gripped my hand tight, bringing me back from my thoughts. 'You turned my life around.'

'Are you coming?' Miraya's voice echoed along with the man's voice, three months ago on this very platform.

My heart was racing. I looked to Kasturi. Miraya paused, looking at me over her shoulder with a smile on her face. Everything slowed down. The only sound for those painful long seconds was the *ba-dum-ba-dum* of my own heartbeat against my eardrums. My eyes looked into Miraya's and again her voice slammed into my soul, leaving me naked and raw in the words.

'*This is not your story*,' she shook her head. 'This is not where you should be, stuck on the platform, yet again. Trust me ...'

Anubhav and Miraya turned and stepped onto the train. My heart swelled as I looked into Kasturi's eyes. This was my story and I knew what I wanted most of all from this life. They disappeared into the coach, and we caught glimpses of them popping in and out through the windows. The metallic caterpillar shouted its last warning, the engine groaning. Chains of doubts were tightening around me, panic engulfing me.

'Go, Shaurya.' Kasturi's sweet voice broke the phantom vices of my doubt.

It wasn't said angrily, and she didn't say it with regret. Kasturi said those words matter-of-factly, and my heart sang knowing that she understood. My throat was too tight with emotions to speak.

Wrapping my arms around her, my lips locked onto hers. Everything melted away and my courage filled me. Her lips were soft and warm against my own. The warmth of her hand caressed my jaw and she was kissing me back, her lips pressing harder. Pulling away, I felt breathless in the moment of the embrace.

'I will love you forever!' I breathed. 'Will you wait for me?'

A tear rolled down her smiling face. 'Yes! But don't give me a forever.'

'Then?'

'Give me an always.'

'Always then,' I grinned, burying my face in her neck and kissing her one last time.

Spinning on my heels, I raced after the train. The coach was rocking; it would be gaining speed in a matter of seconds. Leaping through the door, I swung myself out to look at my lovely Kasturi one more time. She blew me a kiss and I mouthed a *thank you*. She had been right all along when she had said, over a cup of coffee, *You have to have faith in yourself, confidence in who you are and want to be, and be brave enough to take the steps towards achieving your dream.*

I could feel the rumble of the train rolling ever faster on the tracks. Smiling, I rushed down the coach where I found Miraya and Anubhav. One of them looked bewildered to see me, and the other peered up at me with a sense of pride.

She smiled wide and patted the empty seat she had saved for me. 'Glad you could make it.'

Sitting there, the miles grew between me and Jaipur as the train took me closer to Mumbai. The sense of despair and the fears that had kept me in Jaipur felt like distant nightmares. A light filled me and my soul knowing I had taken that leap of faith to achieve my dream. I didn't know what I would tell my parents. But, please, Kasturi, wait for me!

43

Miraya's Diary

We have so much to celebrate right now. As the train lumbers down the track, I think of my last conversation with Mom and Dad when I told them I was returning to Mumbai.

They were so excited, as am I to be seeing my family again. My heart sings with the promises of a future in Mumbai, with Anubhav by my side.

Together, we have strengthened each other and given voice to our own souls.

We know these feelings we have for each other are growing ever stronger. Neither he nor I can portray our emotions, but we both know how much we love each other.

So, I told Mom and Dad that they would be meeting someone very special to me. Actually, two special people, for there is even more to celebrate on this train.

After years of letting his dreams be pushed aside by the story his parents were urging him to write, Shaurya pulled his own book back with both hands today.

Not only did he make the decision to finally step on the train with us, but he also put his feelings into words and told Kasturi that he loved her!

Anubhav and I both felt the love growing, and I know Shaurya had shared his feelings with Anubhav while Kasturi had also told me how she felt. After so much time urging Shaurya to open his heart to her, he finally has.

I feel as if I could float; my heart is so light. The stories of our four lives are interweaving ever more tightly. I could not stop thinking about how the train set a course to change our lives. I took the train to Jaipur and it changed my life. Earlier Anubhav took the train to Bangalore; and now to Mumbai to change his life. And Shaurya, we all know about him!

As much as I will always think fondly of those months spent in Jaipur, I told my parents that I am ready to return to Mumbai. My story takes me in a new direction and I cannot wait to etch the words on paper as each day, every event, unfolds before me.

44

SHAURYA

Mumbai

The sun is brighter, the birds sing longer, and despite the thick city air in Mumbai, I breathed deeper and easier than ever before. Blinking myself awake, I silenced the alarm and stared up at the ceiling. Though I missed my mom, my dad, and Kasturi, I awoke with a smile on my face each morning. My chest rose and fell without the weight of *what could have been*. Rubbing the rest of the sleep from my eyes, I sat up, excited. Today was the first day of my course to be a *filmmaker*.

Miraya had let us stay with her. Her parents didn't mind either. She had a nice apartment with a large guestroom where Anubhav and I stayed. Anubhav had taken the couch. He had insisted on it, reminding me that I knew why I was here and he still had to find his way. As for his drinking, it seemed like a shadow, a dark mark behind him that he no longer needed to wrestle with and lose. He rarely smoked; and often, at the sight of Miraya, he would put it out and go days without even thinking of it again. The expression on his face was like that of a child caught drinking his dad's beer on the patio, and I would laugh when I spotted it.

Mumbai was so different from Jaipur. I thought the streets back home were crowded and busy, but it was a hundred times more intense here. The buildings reached up to the sky three times more than the tallest building in Jaipur, and there were so many of them clustered together. Their shadows cast shade on the streets off and on, but the heat was still thick with the humidity of the day and the salty sweat of the crowds. This place was a hive of faces and people from all walks of life.

My portfolio impressed the college I had aimed to attend. The photography samples I presented to them received highly positive remarks — they said the photographs showed a natural eye for composition and there was a good contrast between the setting and the subject matter.

In the enthusiasm of getting on the train to Mumbai, I had not given a thought that everything I needed was back home. But Mom somehow convinced my dad to give me one chance to follow my dreams. I still don't know how she did that. Maybe she used her magical powers. She also managed to send me a care package with my camera, a few of the photographs she could find, and some essentials. I think it worked in my favour. Snapping some images while exploring Mumbai to build the portfolio gave it a better mix, images from Jaipur interspersing with those of objects they were familiar with living here.

I thought of my mom as I got my things ready for the day. I remembered the sadness in her voice the last time we had spoken.

'I promise you, Mom,' I had told her. 'I'll come back.'

'But when?' she asked, and I could almost sense the tears trailing down her cheeks.

'On the day I am able to meet Dad's eyes once again.'

I shook my head to dissolve the memory of my mom's sad voice.

'Good morning, Shaurya!' Miraya entered the guestroom with three cups of coffee. 'Hope you have an amazing first day.'

'Th-thanks.' Yawning, I picked up a cup for myself. 'Where are you dressed to go so early?'

'Another meeting with a client,' she said. 'Be careful on your way to college, Mumbai is crazy in the morning.'

Anubhav walked in, stretching the aching muscles in his back. 'Good morning everyone.'

'Morning, Anubhav.' Miraya blushed, smiling as she sipped her coffee. 'What do you plan on doing today?'

He sat down, fighting back his yawn before smirking. 'This and that.'

Scoffing, she rolled his eyes. 'I expect an actual answer soon.'

'I know,' he nodded, chuckling. 'If you must know, I've been talking with some colleagues about a new business venture. Nothing solid yet, so I don't want to get my hopes up over nothing.'

'Understandable …' Grabbing her purse, she waved goodbye to us both.

'What sort of business venture?' The coffee was warm and smooth as I sipped it.

'We will see.' Scratching the side of his jaw, Anubhav seemed happy and more lively here in Mumbai. 'I am working on starting my new story, and this time, I am trying my best to include the people in my life. My last story I wrote only for myself and it fell apart, ate me alive. There's no joy in having no one to share your dreams with.'

Staring into my coffee, I could almost see Kasturi staring back at me. 'I agree. A dream should be shared with those you love.'

Looking at the wall clock, he flinched. 'Oh, better get going, Shaurya! You'll never get there in time if you don't!'

I wasted no time in gulping down the rest of my coffee, waking myself completely in preparation for the first day of class. For once, I was looking forward to lectures and endless hours of study. Every minute in Mumbai would be a minute towards making my dream a reality. No longer was I forcing myself down a path to nowhere. The shrieking horns and shouts from the crowds did nothing to shake the positive aura I had woken with, and my smile stayed firm.

The classroom was much like the one back in Jaipur. I couldn't remember the last time I had sat down and pulled out a pen and paper in anticipation of class starting. The professor was younger than the ones I'd had in my CA courses, but he was knowledgeable and I took in every word. There was no need to goad myself to participate; my arm flew to the air to answer questions and again to ask for more knowledge. I lost myself to the lesson unfolding and when the clock landed on the end time, I was heartbroken to have to wait another day to satisfy my hunger.

'You're Shaurya, right?' One of my classmates approached while I was packing up my things, eager to make friends.

I shook his hand. 'Yes, I'm Shaurya.'

'Hi, I'm Vihaan.' He had a sparkle in his eye and I pondered if my eyes were shining so bright as well, living my own dream. 'Where are you from?'

'Jaipur.' My grin widened and I spoke with pride. 'It's been a long-time dream of mine to come to Mumbai to study filmmaking.'

'Wow.' His eyes grew wide. 'That must have been a difficult choice to make …'

Nodding, I zipped up my bag. 'You're right, it was one of the most challenging leaps of faith I have ever taken.'

'What on earth helped you make that jump?' Vihaan's curiosity was growing with each word I spoke. 'It must have been an amazing epiphany of sorts. Tell me your story.'

'Let's go sit and talk over coffee, Vihaan.' This was what being true to yourself, your soul, your heart and dreams felt like; complete bliss. 'Let me tell you my story ...'

45

Anubhav

As Shaurya pursued his dreams, I followed mine as well.

At first I was hesitant to return to the career path that I had thrown away as I let the devastation of my parents' death tear me apart. But Miraya helped me along, softly nudging me forward when doubts encroached.

With Miraya's encouragement, I began to slowly rebuild my career. I pitched a new idea to some investors and the chances of securing the funding were looking good.

My love for Miraya grew every passing day and I didn't let a day go by without telling her so.

'You made a man out of a monster,' I said one day. 'It's the magic of your true love.'

'That's what love does,' she responded, hugging me tightly. 'It makes us better.'

'You make us better,' I said.

Miraya frowned. 'No, Anubhav. *We* made *us*. This is

not all because of me. You put your feet back on the ground when you were afraid to go on. At any point after that horrible day at Amer Fort, you could have given up. But you kept fighting. I am proud of you,' she said.

'You are so good for me,' I breathed.

She smiled softly. 'I don't know if my words still have the power to heal you or my love still has the power to inspire you. But I'm with you always and you'll always have me.'

Our foreheads touched as I let her feel the love radiating from me. 'I will always look forward to the next day, because I know you'll be there with me and it will be so beautiful.'

One day, she gave me a beautifully wrapped present. My mind raced — it wasn't my birthday ... was it an anniversary that I had missed?

'What is this for?' I asked, my fingers pulling at the white ribbon curled around the present.

'Open it,' she commanded. 'Maybe it's silly, but ...'

At that, I tore the paper off the present and absently balled it up, shoving the colourful wrapping in my pocket.

In my hands was a simple, humble notebook.

I flipped through the blank pages and then my eyes met her dancing ones.

'Some stories are hidden deep within you. You just need to find them,' she explained. 'I thought you might want to start writing in your own journal.'

That night, after Miraya had kissed me goodnight, I flipped on the light to the small patio in the guestroom. Shrugging into a jacket to ward off the cold, I picked up the notebook and slipped outside.

What should I write for the one who gave words to my life? I sat for the longest time, my pen rolling between my fingers. Then I began …

For a moment, forget who you are. More importantly, leave behind who we are and empty out everything. Instead, just be me.

'I never wanted anything from life.'

If I say those words, I would be lying. In fact, that would be the biggest lie of my life. I wanted, I have always wanted. I just never could bring the words out. My voice failing, my heart breaking, my soul shattering.

But, what do I really want in life?

I don't know yet. So, I will tell you everything I wanted and still want. Today, I will be true; true to you, and most importantly, true to myself.

I … I … I want to live.

Yes. Not one but many lives in one lifetime. I want to write about myself and everyone I ever met, capture the essence of what it's like to live. To be able to read everything beautiful and painful ever written and appreciate the experiences captured. All of this hoping to inspire and be inspired.

I want to learn and to teach. Yes, both, because I have

had life-defining encounters that need to be shared and understood. Even so, I still have life-changing experiences, lessons to learn.

I want to give away everything I have. Yes, I want that and I want to begin again. To remind myself what it means to start over, to be back at the beginning of one's life.

I want to eat and dress well, have a nice car and a nicer home. To be rich, famous and appreciated. The little things and the bigger things, I want all of them.

I want to be single and yet attached. Alone yet accompanied. I want to be everything and nothing, all at once!

I want Death to want me. He cannot take me, I want him to come when I have exhausted these lives I want to live and become! I want him to desire the enriched soul I will be!

I want it all; slowly, gradually, definitely. But is this all possible? Can one person be all these things in one lifetime?

I don't know, but I certainly want to know.

THREE YEARS LATER

EPILOGUE

SHAURYA

Jaipur

The train groaned and creaked to a stop, its whistle blowing to announce my arrival. I took in a deep breath. The passengers before me poured out as if coffee beans funnelled through a grinder. The first familiar faces I would see since I'd left for Mumbai to pursue being a filmmaker were my parents. I followed the crowd I found myself in until I was out and away from the train. As the bodies around me dispersed, I saw that, there at the bench, were my parents.

My mom rushed through the last of the crowd, her warm arms hugging me tight. She felt lighter, more fragile in my arms. I couldn't help but wonder what signs of age my own face showed in just three years' time.

'I have missed you so much, Shaurya!' Her voice shook

with excitement at seeing me again. 'It's good to have you home again!'

Smiling, I stepped back to look at her beaming face. 'I have missed you too.'

My eyes went past her shoulder where my dad cleared his throat. I took a few steps towards him and bowed to touch his feet. When I'd left Jaipur, I'd gone against his advice. There was no way to know if he felt shame, anger, or even sad over the action I'd taken so close to the CA final exams. I could feel his eyes on me and I willed myself to look up. A smiling face greeted me. He held out a hand and he brought me back upright before giving me a firm handshake.

'I am proud of you, Shaurya.' His eyes were watery, but never did a tear grace his cheek. 'You were brave to chase after a dream like that.'

'Th-thank you.' I had no other words.

Again, he cleared his throat. 'I'm sorry I ever doubted your resolve to achieve your dream.'

My chest swelled with pride to hear my dad say those words about a path I'd chosen for myself. He had said once, *It's a fool's dream,* but here he stood before me with pride. Seeing their reactions was soothing, but my mind was on who I would be seeing next.

'Do you mind if I have a guest over for dinner tonight?' I asked, my arm wrapped around my mom's shoulders as we walked side-by-side out of the railway station.

'Absolutely!' she chuckled, leaning her head into me. 'Oh, I will have more than enough food cooked to celebrate your achievements and you coming home!'

More than anything, I wanted to see Kasturi. She had promised to wait for me and even now, her kiss tingled on my lips. Three years was a long time to keep such a promise.

Her last phone call to me was so optimistic, so happy. While she was anxious for me to return to Jaipur, she said, she was so very happy that I had found the courage and the faith to go to Mumbai to chase my dreams.

She had used our time apart following the other part of her story. She had worked hard at college and completed her MBA. Now, working in an MNC, she was anxious for us to merge our two paths and continue to make our dreams come true together.

I couldn't wait either.

My parents headed for our flat and I did everything I could not to run to Kasturi's door. Knocking on the door, my joints ached with excitement.

'Shaurya?' The voice was not the one I dreamed of every night, but instead it was Kasturi's mom. 'Oh, you're back!'

'Hi, Aunty. I was looking for Kasturi?' My smile was dropping, unsure of the answer I would receive.

'The terrace,' her mom smiled, patting my shoulder. 'She might still be there.'

'Wh-where?' I blinked.

She was turning me around and leading me off the stoop, laughing. 'She visits the terrace every day since you left, now go!'

My heart pounded against my chest. Without even thinking, I found myself running to the terrace, eager to find Kasturi. The thudding of my feet against the terrace floor brought me to a stop. I looked around, trying to catch my breath. Peering around, my heart was in my throat. The sunlight twinkled across the plants like miniature spotlights on actors on a terracotta stage. Standing up straight, I took in a deep breath, stilling my panic. No one was there. Groaning, I covered my face, wondering how long ago she'd been here. Had I come here first, would I have seen her?

'Shaurya?'

Kasturi's voice made my soul sing. I looked over my shoulder, and there she stood, with tear-filled eyes. I had run past her in my excitement. We stood, our eyes shouting our feelings louder than any words could ever do in an eternity. The blood in my veins spurred my voice into action.

'Kasturi!'

We closed the gap, neither of us able to hide our excitement in seeing one another after three long years. Wrapping my arms around her, I spun her around and laughter erupted from us. Her feet landed on the ground and her hot hands held my cheeks as she pressed her lips to mine. The feeling of the first kiss at the railway station came back to life. Gripping her shoulders, I broke the sweet moment; there was so much I still needed to tell her, show her.

'How are you, Shaurya?' Her eyes were more beautiful than ever, her palms warm against my cheeks.

'I am just like you, Kasturi. Why didn't you come to the station?' My fingers slid a locket of her hair from her brow as I fell deeper into the flecks of brown and gold that made up her irises.

'I wanted you to have your time with your parents,' she said slowly, looking deep in my eyes.

'And what are you doing here?' I asked, trying to read her eyes.

She blushed, a train hooting in the distance. 'I watch the trains, thinking of you …'

My own face reddened, my cheeks aching with a smile as I handed her an envelope. Her hand rubbed the front where the words in elegant calligraphy read, *This is My Story*. She opened the envelope with growing anticipation, recognizing the handwriting. Opening the card, she read as quickly as she could. I watched as her lips mouthed the words silently, her eyes sparkling with each word reflected in her pupils.

'Miraya and Anubhav …' she shrieked, hugging me, '… are getting married!'

'Yes! And Anubhav is hosting a grand party to celebrate the success of his new startup along with the wedding,' I said, gently pulling her off me so I could continue what I had come here to do. I handed her a spiral-bound book. Gripping it in her delicate hands, she read the title aloud — *This is Not Your Story* — and flipped through the pages.

'I have finished writing my first movie and have approached some producers. They have loved it, and if everything falls in place, I might be directing it soon!'

Kasturi stood their speechless, looking deep in my eyes. Then, smiling, she tried to hug me once more, but instead I dropped to one knee. There was one last chapter I still needed in my story. I opened the tiny box I'd brought with me, the sunlight sending the diamond flashing. The reflection off the ring danced in her eyes and I etched her expression to memory.

'Kasturi, will you marry me? Will you be the part of my story? Will you make my story worth telling?'

'YES!' Kasturi fell into my arms, our lips greeting one another, and she whispered into my ear, 'Yes, Shaurya!'

THANK YOU

To My Readers,

Thank you for joining me in the telling of the story of Shaurya, Miraya and Anubhav. I hope they touched your soul the same way they touched mine.

To the ones who write encouraging emails or speak to me in person on the road — your feedback means the world to me. Thank you!

To the ones who enjoy my books and pass on copies to friends, relatives and neighbours, you are multiplying the impact of the books. Thank you!

To the ones who write passionately negative reviews — your feedback challenges me to write more effectively in the future. Thank you!

Thank you for interacting with me, sharing your lives with me, and being the reason I can continue doing what I love.

If you loved this book and have a minute to spare, I would really appreciate a short review on the site where you bought the book. Your help in spreading the word will be greatly appreciated.

You're all amazing!

With profound gratitude,
Savi

Acknowledgements

I am an author, you are a reader and I created this story, these characters, these heroes for you. But this would not have been possible without all the backstage heroes, the characters who complete the story of Savi Sharma. So, I would like to thank them here.

First and above all, I praise the Universe for guiding me towards the purpose of my life.

My family and friends, for their love, support and trust in me.

My cute little neighbour, Kush, for entertaining and amusing me with his innocent acts.

Special thanks to Deepthi Talwar, my sweet editor, for saving me the embarrassment of making terrible mistakes.

I am grateful to the entire team at Westland Ltd., led by Gautam Padmanabhan, for their untiring efforts in helping my stories reach you.

And finally, I know that you did not want to be named, my best friend and mentor, Ashish Bagrecha — without your efforts and encouragements, I would not have become the storyteller I am today, and I understand how difficult it was for you, therefore, I can just say thanks for everything and hope the Universe gives you all the best in return. I and my readers are waiting for your story. Please write soon!

SAVI SHARMA is a simple girl from Surat who left her CA studies to become a storyteller. She self-published her inspirational novel *Everyone Has a Story*, which was acquired later by Westland Ltd. More than 100,000 copies of her debut novel sold in less than four months, making it India's fastest-selling debut novel. *This Is Not Your Story* is the second step in her mission to inspire and touch millions of lives.

She is also co-founder of the motivational media blog 'Life & People', where she writes about the law of attraction, positivity, spirituality, travelling and storytelling.

She loves observing people in cafés, where she often searches for her stories. She has a secret list of a hundred wishes which she wants to fulfil in this one lifetime.

You can connect with her on www.savisharma.com or follow @storytellersavi on Facebook, Twitter and Instagram.